PRAISE FOR THE FIERY TALES

"Evocative, erotic. . . [A] sensual treat!"
— **Sylvia Day**,
#1 *New York Times* bestselling author

"Hot enough to warm the coldest winter night."
— **Publishers Weekly**

"Sophisticated and deeply romantic."
—**Elizabeth Hoyt**,
New York Times bestselling author

"Sure to delight!"
— **Jennifer Ashley**,
New York Times bestselling author

"The most luscious, sexy take on classic fairy tales I've ever read!"
—**Cheryl Holt**,
New York Times bestselling author

"Sets the classic fairy tale(s) ablaze!"
—**Anna Campbell**,
bestselling, award-winning author

Little Red Writing

A Fiery Tale

LILA DIPASQUA

DiPasqua

Excerpt from *Bewitching in Boots*, by Lila DiPasqua copyright © Lila DiPasqua
Cover Design by Carrie Divine/Seductive Designs

Photography of Couple by Period Images;
Background by FairytaleDesign
(Małgorzata Patrzyk)/Depositphotos.com

Interior Design by Woven Red Author Services, www.WovenRed.ca

PRINTING HISTORY
First Edition: From *Awakened by a Kiss*, Berkley Sensation/Penguin Group (USA) Inc.—August 2010
Second Edition: Lila DiPasqua—April 2016

ISBN: 978-0-9880350-9-6 (trade pbk)
ISBN: 978-0-9880350-8-9 (e-book)

To Lynda Simmons and Margie Lawson.
Two brilliant women who taught me so much.

And to Karen Brown who, years ago, generously opened her
home to a group of writers every week for several months.
Those classes started me down this path.
I miss those evenings and our groups!

Little Red Writing

Moral of the Story of Little Red Riding Hood:

"One sees here that young children,
Especially pretty girls,
Who're bred as pure as pearls,
Should question words addressed by men.
Or they may serve one day as feast
For a wolf or other beast.
I say a wolf since not all are wild
Or are indeed the same in kind.
For some are winning and have sharp minds,
Some are loud, smooth or mild.
Others appear plain kind or unriled.
They follow young ladies wherever they go,
Right into the halls of their very own homes.
Alas, for those girls who've refused the truth:
The sweetest tongue has the sharpest tooth."

Charles Perrault (1628–1703)

CHAPTER ONE

France 1685

"Who is *he?*" Just as the question tumbled from Anne's mouth, the man in the light gray justacorps disappeared into the crowd. Again.

Her sister Henriette glanced over her shoulder. As usual, the Comtesse de Cottineau's Saturday Salon was filled to overflowing. Though their patroness had been called away due to a family emergency, she'd insisted that Anne and her sisters carry on with the popular weekly event in her absence. Aristos and literati who frequented her home had been admitted and were presently milling about.

Henriette turned back. "Who?"

Who indeed.

Anne was the last person to be taken in by a handsome face, but she couldn't stop herself from trying to locate the man with the disarming gray eyes. Smoky eyes that had locked with hers for several seconds and quickened her pulse. A stunning reaction on her part. Unprecedented, actually. Twice he'd drawn her attention out of the masses straight to him by doing nothing more than directing his smoldering gaze her way. Once, even when she was engaged in a fascinating discussion about Spanish literature with the Marquis de Musis. Both times the beautiful dark-haired stranger had been at a distance in a different part of the Great Room, but she felt the heat of his regard long before she spotted him.

Maddeningly, he kept vanishing into the sea of faces.

Dragging her gaze back to Henriette, Anne noticed her sister's curious expression.

"A gentleman," Anne responded. "I've never seen him before. We should welcome him, but I seem to have lost him in the crowd." She felt foolish. Stepping into the Comtesse's shoes and acting as hostess to her elite guests was daunting. Unnerving. Her jangled nerves were likely the reason for her peculiar reaction. Statesmen, lords and ladies were in attendance along with some of the most respected scholars, writers and dramatists.

Social biases set aside while under the Comtesse's roof, they gathered together each week to debate and discuss language and literature, history and philosophy.

It was thrilling. A place of enlightenment. A great honor to be in among such distinguished company. Such brilliant minds. To be part of Madame de Cottineau's Salon—one of the city's most prestigious. Born into minor nobility, with little by way of social influence and finances, Anne and her two sisters would not have been welcome had the Comtesse not taken an interest in their humble writings and agreed to sponsor their works.

But today's Saturday Salon was different. And it wasn't simply because the Comtesse was missing. Or that Anne and her sisters, Henriette and Camille, were hostesses.

It was because of a single man. A most unsettling, mysterious gentleman.

Anne and her sisters owed much to Madame de Cottineau. Making her guests feel welcome while she was away was the least they could do for her. Yet the gentleman with the disquieting gray eyes was making the task even more challenging for Anne. She should have greeted him the moment she saw him, but the impact he'd had on her unbalanced her. She lost her nerve to approach him, when courage was never something she lacked.

Henriette's gaze swept the room. "What does he look like?"

His face appeared in her mind's eye. Anne felt her cheeks warm. Dear God, she was *blushing*. And if that wasn't embarrassing enough, she was at a complete loss for words. She was a writer, and yet she couldn't conjure a phrase to adequately describe the sheer male perfection she'd seen. Not without sounding as awestruck as she felt. Like some smitten ingénue.

"Madame de Pierpont?" Upon hearing someone call Henriette's name, Anne was yanked from her thoughts. The Comtesse d'Azan approached and looped arms with Henriette. "Excuse me for interrupting, but the Baron de Lenoncourt has brought up the subject of the Latin classics. Come join in the discussion. You have such an interesting take on the topic."

Henriette glanced at Anne.

"Oh, you must come, too, Mademoiselle de Vignon," Comtesse d'Azan said to Anne. "You are the only one who can keep the Baron focused on one topic at a time." Softly, she laughed.

Anne smiled at the gracious comment and was about to respond when something, or rather someone, caught her eye. Over the Comtesse's shoulder, there at the back of the room, was the mysterious man.

His eyes captured hers and held her riveted, the corner of his mouth lifting into a sensual smile. Her stomach fluttered wildly. The crowd shifted and he disappeared from her seeking sight, instantly snapping the spell he'd cast. Anne tamped down her ire.

Enough was enough.

It galled her that she was behaving so foolishly. She knew better. She knew the damage an attractive man could cause a woman's mind, heart and spirit.

"Madame, I would love to join you," Anne said, grasping her skirts. "But first, there is a matter I must attend to. Please excuse me." Anne turned into the throng and made her way toward the back corner where she'd last seen the enigmatic stranger.

A smile firmly in place, she moved through the crowd, exchanging brief pleasantries along the way, behaving as any cordial hostess should. Just as soon as she located the man with the silvery eyes, she intended to extend him every courtesy. She'd welcome him to the Comtesse de Cottineau's home. And respond to him no differently than to any other guest present.

So why were her insides still quivering?

*****

"She approaches. What do you think, Nicolas, is she the one?" Thomas, Comte de Gamory, asked near Nicolas's ear.

Nicolas de Savignac studied the woman in the blue gown as she made her way through the mass.

Anne de Vignon. The middle sister.

He'd overheard one of the guests point her out. Thanks to the sheer numbers in the room, he could easily hide in plain sight and observe her and her two siblings. Allowing them to see him only when he wished it.

Anne's bright red curls lightly swept her bare shoulders each time she turned her head to acknowledge one of the guests. The color of her hair was extraordinary. He was gripped by a powerful urge to run his fingers through the fiery-colored locks.

She wasn't at all what he'd expected a spinster poetess to look like. He was expecting someone rather plain. This woman was ravishing. The extent of her allure, a surprise. As was the bolt of heat that shot through his veins and tightened his groin the moment their gazes met.

He didn't like surprises.

He was still reeling over the fact that their investigation had led him to *this* hôtel, of all places. To the home of one of his very own relatives.

Discreetly, Anne glanced here and there. It was obvious to him, if no one else, that she was hunting for him. What she didn't know was that he was the one doing the hunting. That he was relentless in his pursuits, cunning enough to earn the nickname *le Loup*—the Wolf.

And he was here to catch his prey.

"Nicolas?"

He pulled his gaze from the redheaded beauty back to Thomas. His friend was frowning. It took some getting used to, seeing him out of his Musketeer uniform and in formal attire. Or in being out of uniform himself. But to walk in wearing the distinct blue tabard would have alerted everyone, especially the sisters in question, that he and Thomas were part of the King's elite private Guard. Newly promoted, Nicolas intended to prove to his King, his Captain, and the rest of the men that he deserved the honored position. That he could be as good a Musketeer, if not better, than his late legendary brother, David—Musketeer extraordinaire. Nicolas had, after all, easily beaten out other highly qualified noblemen for one of the coveted few spots. On his own. By *his* skill. *His* abilities. Just as he expected to. Once he set his mind on attaining a goal, he was unstoppable. And nothing was going to keep him from successfully completing this mission—a mission His Majesty wanted kept most quiet and accomplished posthaste.

"Well?" Thomas asked. "What do you think? Is it her or one of her other two sisters?"

Nicolas gazed once again at his object of interest. Anne had stopped and was speaking to a group of ladies.

"I don't know." *Merde.* How he wished he did. From the information he'd gathered, Anne de Vignon was the author of two volumes of poetry. He'd read them both. He'd read all the books the three sisters had written. Each woman had a distinct writing style—dark, romantic, humorous—and yet, he still wasn't certain who wielded the poisonous pen.

Now that Anne was closer, he could better appreciate the womanly details of her form. No doubt about it, both far and near, she was comely in the extreme. Her gown, though not as costly as the others in the room, accentuated her curves in the most delectable way. With the discerning eye of a libertine, he took note of her creamy skin, the slight blush to her cheeks, and the rise and fall of her breasts, her breathing a bit too quick, belying her mask of composure.

Under the unruffled façade she was discomposed. And it was because of him.

There had definitely been a mutual attraction. He'd seen it in her eyes. If used correctly, it could be a delicious advantage. He wasn't above using whatever means necessary to uncover the identity of the anonymous author who wrote under the nom de plume, Gilbert Leduc.

"She is beautiful," Thomas murmured. "I don't know about you, Nicolas, but I'd rather fuck a woman who looks like that, than arrest her."

"You'll not touch her." *Dieu*, that sounded absurdly possessive.

Thomas chuckled. "So you've set your sights on Anne, *le Loup*? Poor woman. She doesn't stand a chance. Curious, why her? Why not one of the other two sisters?" He gave a nod in their general direction. Both were on the opposite side of the room, engrossed in conversation. "They're comely, too."

Indeed. All three sisters had the same beautiful fiery-colored hair. Henriette de Pierpont was the eldest and the only one to marry. Widowed four years, she was attractive in her own right. As was the youngest, Mademoiselle Camille de Vignon.

But there was something about Anne . . .

"We're here to discover which sister is the author of the pen portraits and bring her before His Majesty. As ordered. Whichever will confess to the truth is the one I'm interested in," Nicolas said. Those who were patrons of the arts and had enough coin couldn't collect unsanctioned books fast enough.

Nicolas had uncovered the underground press that was printing the illegal volumes of short stories. He and Thomas had spent weeks surreptitiously watching the Parisian publisher, observing the comings and goings at his print shop, and following messenger boys until Nicolas was finally led to the home of the Comtesse de Cottineau—and the three authors who resided there.

Everyone was talking about the anonymously written stories. Everyone had a strong opinion on what should be done about the author. The women praised the writer. The men, especially those who were the subject of ridicule in the published tales, clamored for justice.

Pen portraits were nothing new. Many writers used real people—mostly members of the upper class—as characters in their books. Names were changed, but the author always made it easy to identify the person being portrayed by the fictitious character. Characters that were always written with a flattering slant. However, the author of *these* pen portraits did just the opposite. This author maligned and mocked men. Important men. Powerful men. Mercilessly. It was out of control.

Anne stepped away from the women and continued on, getting nearer, her lovely dark eyes still searching for him. Unable to spot him.

His lips twitched as he held back his smile. *That's it. Come closer, pretty rabbit.*

It had taken some doing, but he'd managed to get the Comtesse de Cottineau out of her home, sending the old crone far away under false pretenses. He despised the woman. Had held nothing but contempt for her his entire life, and with her out of the hôtel, nothing stood between him and the three redheaded females.

He was focused. Ready.

The trap was set.

*****

He wasn't there. At the back corner of the room, Anne turned to face the crowd. She scanned the Great Room but couldn't locate the mysterious gentleman anywhere.

"Pardon, mademoiselle."

She jumped at the sound of the male voice behind her and spun around.

Vincent, the majordomo, gave a short bow. "Your pardon. I didn't mean to startle you." Tall, thin, his hair completely white, Vincent always had the same expressionless look upon his face. A longtime loyal servant to the Comtesse, he'd been unnerving to Anne from the time she and her sisters moved in last spring. She could never decipher his emotions or what he was thinking.

"That's all right, Vincent."

"Mademoiselle, the Comte de Gamory and the Comte de Lambelle are here."

"Oh?"

"They have requested a private moment. They're in the Mercury drawing room. Monsieur de Lambelle has asked to see your sisters as well. Mademoiselle Camille de Vignon has already excused herself and is presently there."

Anne frowned. "Vincent, we cannot all excuse ourselves and disappear. What about the Comtesse's guests? Who are these men?" She'd never heard of them.

"Nicolas de Savignac, Comte de Lambelle, is related to the Comtesse, mademoiselle."

She raised her brows. Her patroness? *He is?*

"Yes, mademoiselle. He is her grandson and wishes to speak to you."

CHAPTER TWO

Anne opened the door to the Mercury drawing room and stepped inside. Her heart lurched.

The mysterious man.

He was seated across from Camille with another gentleman to his left. The moment those gray eyes touched upon her, his tactile gaze sent a rush of heat low in her belly.

Get hold of yourself. She wasn't easily rattled, but *he* was rattling her in the most shocking ways. It defied logic. He was a perfect stranger. Yet there was nothing logical about it.

It was all physical.

Anne took in a fortifying breath before she approached.

He rose to his full height and moved toward her, pure masculine grace in motion, getting closer with each wild beat of her heart. By the time he stood before her, he wore the same half-smile on his handsome face as before.

Tilting her chin, Anne gazed up at him. Good Lord. He was even more devastating to behold up close.

"This is my sister, Anne de Vignon," Camille said, having approached without Anne noticing. She was too busy being ridiculously entranced by the tall attractive man before her. "Anne, this is the Comte de Lambelle—Nicolas de Savignac. He is our dear Comtesse's grandson."

Dear God, *he* was the grandson?

His smile broadened. Taking her hand—one she hadn't yet offered, her arms still dangling foolishly at her sides—he pressed his warm lips against it. Tiny tingles shot up her arm and rippled down her spine.

"Enchanté," he said, his voice rich and seductive.

Stop staring. Where are your manners? Say something.

"A pleasure to meet you, Monsieur le Comte," she said, sounding slightly breathless. This man was dangerous, his appeal far too compelling. Her every instinct warned her to stay far away.

"Please, no titles or formality are necessary. Call me Nicolas. May I call you Anne?"

She glanced at her younger sister Camille and caught the sobering sight of her smitten expression. Camille's regard was directed at the other gentleman in the room. Clearly her sister was behaving as uncharacteristically as she was.

She prayed *she* didn't look like that.

Returning her attention to the Comtesse's grandson, she responded, "Anne would be fine." Only because she was trying to be gracious toward her patroness's kin did she cede to his request, though permitting such familiarity made her uneasy.

Pleased by her answer, Nicolas's smile grew. He gestured to the gentleman beside him—a man of similar age yet slighter build. "Allow me to introduce my cousin Thomas, Comte de Gamory."

Anne's greeting of the Comte de Gamory—or rather "Thomas" as he preferred—was much better.

"Forgive our intrusion into your get-together. I had no idea there would be so many guests present," Nicolas said, his smile slowly diminishing on his face. Then, lowering his chin, briefly he shook his head. When his gray eyes met hers once more, they looked saddened. "This is yet another example of how little I know my own grandmother, I fear. I had no idea she had weekly salons—a fact Camille was kind enough to relay."

Their patroness was a strong-willed woman, the center of attention at any gathering. Never afraid of voicing her opinion.

But when it came to personal matters, such as family, she'd been silent. The Comtesse had never mentioned grandchildren and only once indicated she'd had any children at all. A son and a daughter. There were obvious familial strains in the Comtesse's family.

"I understand from your sister that the Comtesse isn't here." Nicolas's expression was rueful.

"Yes, that's true," Anne regretted having to say. "She's been called away. A letter arrived from her sister last week. She's gone to see her."

"We did inquire if there was anything amiss," Camille added. "But she wouldn't say one way or the other."

Nicolas looked at his cousin and, with a sigh, placed a hand on the man's shoulder. "How very disappointing. We've missed her. I had so hoped to surprise her."

Thomas nodded, looking not quite as aggrieved. "Indeed, cousin. I know how much you have wanted to make amends with your grandmother."

"*His* grandmother?" Anne asked. "Is she not yours as well?"

Thomas's eyes widened and all that escaped his lips was, "*Ah* . . . well—"

"No," Nicolas interjected. "Thomas is my cousin from my father's side. My late mother was the Comtesse's daughter. Thomas is as dear to me as a brother. In fact, I lost my brother not long ago. It was then that I decided I needed to make changes in my life. One of which is trying to forge a relationship with a grandmother who has been all but a stranger to me."

"Yes, yes. That's true," Thomas concurred with a nod.

Nicolas de Savignac had had his share of unfortunate losses. The notion tugged at Anne's heart. "I see. My condolences, Monsieur de—"

"Nicolas, please," he amended.

"*Nicolas* . . . my condolences for the loss of your mother and brother. And to you, too, Thomas—for the loss of your cousin and aunt."

"My condolences, as well—to both of you." Camille said, her brown eyes mirroring the sympathy in her tone.

"Thank you, my ladies. We appreciate your kindness." Nicolas looked at his cousin. "Don't we, Thomas?"

"Hmm? Oh. Yes. Indeed, we do."

"I'm equally sorry to hear of your estrangement with your grandmother," Anne said. "We have been living with her for a year and find her to be a most delightful spirited lady who has a great passion for the arts."

"That, too, is something I was unaware of, Anne," Nicolas said.

She liked the way he said her name. She liked it too much. Why, when he uttered it, did it have such a heated effect on her senses?

"Camille tells us that you are both writers. I had no idea my grandmother had such lovely, fascinating ladies living in her home." Nicolas's sensual half-smile returned.

Thomas offered a smile as well. "Yes. Having you ladies here, of all places, was definitely a . . . surprise."

"A good surprise, I hope," Camille remarked shamelessly, ignoring the look of disapproval Anne discreetly flashed her. These men were of rank, and—albeit estranged—nonetheless relations of their patroness. Two very strong reasons not to flirt—no matter how innocently done. Camille knew better. She knew to be cautious around men in the noble class. Knew what some of them were capable of.

"A most delightful surprise, Camille," Nicolas assured.

Anne had to admit, the man's manners were polished and he was charming in the extreme. Not to mention that his proximity had every nerve ending in her body humming with awareness.

More reasons to keep a distance.

"Our other sister, Henriette, is a writer as well," Camille said, her approval of Nicolas's response evident by her jubilant expression. "She has penned some wonderful stories."

Anne glanced at the door. "Henriette must be caught up in conversation. We really must return to the Comtesse's guests.

Her Salon means a great deal to her, so much so that she didn't want to cancel it in her absence. My apologies for Henriette—"

Nicolas raised a hand. "No need to apologize. Thomas and I arrived quite unexpectedly."

"Please, join us," Camille said. "We'll introduce you to your grandmother's friends."

"That is very gracious of you, Camille," Nicolas said. "In fact, I wish to learn as much as I can about my grandmother, but our trip from Varise was a lengthy one. We're terribly exhausted. I hope you understand if we decline?"

Anne was more than a tad relieved, needing space between her and the far-too-attractive Nicolas de Savignac. "Of course. I'll ask Vincent to show you to your rooms, where you can rest and refresh yourselves." The faster she left the room, the sooner her pulse would return to normal.

"Will you be staying awhile?" Anne disliked the hopeful tone in Camille's voice and immediately worried about the answer.

"Having come all this way," Nicolas responded, "I don't wish to leave without seeing my grandmother. I've heard her sister is a robust woman in both health and form. I have a feeling the Comtesse will return soon enough. Until then, Thomas and I will be staying, and I shall anxiously await her arrival." He smiled.

Anne's stomach dropped.

He could be here *weeks*. Oh, this was bad. Very bad. Especially since she found the notion as appealing as it was disquieting.

His light-colored eyes moved to Anne as he said, "There will be plenty of time to get to know each other."

*****

Nicolas listened to the retreating footsteps of the two Vignon sisters from behind the drawing room's closed doors. Only when he could no longer hear the sound of heels clicking against marble did he grin, saunter over to a chair and drop into it.

"Nicolas," Thomas said, dragging a chair over to him and sitting down. "You are in the wrong profession, my friend. You should take to the stage. That was quite a performance you gave."

Still smiling, Nicolas propped his boots on a nearby settee and linked his fingers behind his head. "It worked, didn't it? We have their sympathy. Moreover, we have unfettered access to the hôtel and the lovely authors who live in it."

"Well, I am not the actor you are. If you are going to surprise me—such as making me your 'cousin'—please give me forewarning."

In a good mood, Nicolas simply chuckled. "Do not fret, Thomas. You did fine. And we will do more than fine with this mission. A handful of days, perhaps even less, and I'll know which sister is Gilbert Leduc, make my arrest, and impress the King."

It was Thomas's turn to smile. "You have hardly been in the Guard for long. You're not hunting for a promotion already, are you, *le Loup*?"

"Of course." It had taken some finagling, but he'd convinced his Captain, Tristan de Tiersonnier, to select him for the mission. How was he to catch the eye of the King if he didn't do things that made him stand out? The mission was one others had failed at. Leduc had been ever so elusive. "I intend one day to be Captain of His Majesty's private Guard—the King's most trusted protector. Keeping your eye toward promotion is the only way to excel."

"*Captain of the Guard?*" Thomas laughed. "You do aim high. Not even your brother achieved that."

That decimated his jovial spirits. Any references that remotely suggested he wasn't as good as his brother had that effect. "I am not like David." He was better than David. He was a better fencer. A better loser when bested by his brother. A more gracious winner when Nicolas did the besting—and never, not ever, did he gloat. Pitting his sons against each other all their lives, their father encouraged constant competition between them, fueling their lifelong rivalry. And even though David and their father were both dead, Nicolas still wouldn't—couldn't—

stop until he'd proved to himself and his superiors that he was in no way a lesser version of his older sibling.

"How do you plan on discovering which sister is Gilbert Leduc?"

Pulling his feet off the settee and placing them back onto the floor, Nicolas leaned toward his friend, his smile returning. "Anne is going to tell me."

"You think you can get her to talk?"

"I'm certain of it." The air between them practically sizzled and crackled with hot carnal awareness. He'd never admit to Thomas just how strongly she was playing havoc with his libido. She had him stiff as a spike the entire time they'd spoken, hungry for the taste of her mouth and her tantalizing nipples that were so obviously hard and pressing against the bodice of her gown.

"What makes you so certain?" Thomas asked. "Because she is—if the look in her eyes was any indication—attracted to you?"

"Precisely."

"And how are you going to attain the information from her? By fucking the answer out of her?"

Nicolas sat back in his chair. "Now you see the added appeal to this mission."

Thomas laughed and shook his head. "It doesn't bother you that you'd be bedding the lady one moment, then possibly—if she turns out to be Leduc—arresting her the next?"

"If she is the author—Gilbert Leduc—then she has broken the law by using an illegal press and writing unsanctioned, not to mention defamatory, literature. If Leduc turns out to be one of her sisters, I've no doubt she's assisting in some capacity in her sibling's criminal endeavors. Either way, she is guilty. I have no qualms about doing my duty, and neither should you. We are expected to succeed in our mission. If the lady offers up some decadent delights before all is said and done," Nicolas shrugged, "I'll not refuse her." No man would. Not a woman as beautiful as Anne de Vignon.

He'd seen lustful interest in the eyes of many of the men at the Salon. Did she have a lover among them? The possibility that he'd have competition didn't worry him. He'd have Anne, his instincts telling him that beneath her cool proper layers, he'd find passion. Fire. A woman sure to offer a man untold carnal bliss.

"And what about your grandmother? She is mixed up in all this," Thomas said. "As their patroness, her funding has made it possible for these women to write and publish sanctioned—and one of them, unsanctioned—literature. This 'Gilbert Leduc' matter will backlash on her."

"My grandmother is an uncompromising woman who is devoid of compassion." Nicolas couldn't keep the caustic tone from dripping off his words. "I have no doubt she's played a very important role in this smear campaign. Should the King decide to punish her, she has no one to blame but herself." He had no sympathy where the old woman was concerned. Though he'd not expected to discover his own grandmother involved in this sordid mess, he wasn't going to let that deter him in any way. Absurd as it was, the only thing that was truly bothering him was that he'd been correct in his assumption: his grandmother hadn't spoken of him, or likely his mother, either. That fact was evident by the looks on Anne's and Camille's faces. It was obvious they never knew he existed. Though the Comtesse's silence helped with his plan, he disliked that the notion had any sting at all. After all these years, he shouldn't care a whit that the heartless hag had disowned his mother—turning her back on her own daughter—and never had any interest in her grandsons, treating them all as if they were dead.

"I've read Gilbert Leduc's writings," Nicolas said, shoving the past aside. "I believe the author we seek is a woman scorned. Someone whose anger has spilled over onto the male gender at large. A man or men—past or present—have inspired her to write telltale stories that humiliate men and besmirch their reputations."

"So you think the author is using these pen portraits as a method of revenge?" Thomas asked.

"I do."

"Perhaps she simply does it for funds? With the wild popularity of the anthologies, surely it's been a lucrative venture for her?"

"Indeed, Thomas. The money is likely a motivating factor. But I think the underlying reason why she does this is much more personal. The eldest sister, Henriette de Pierpont, was once married. Let's learn as much as we can about her marriage, and in particular, her deceased husband's treatment of her." Nicolas rose, suddenly feeling fatigued, intent on seeking out the old servant and retiring to his room. "Camille de Vignon seems to have an interest in you, Thomas. Speak to her. See what you can learn. I'll focus on Anne," he said as his friend rose from his chair. "I'll be with her every minute of the day."

And each night—if all went according to plan.

This mission was going to be easy.

*****

"I don't like this. Not one bit," Henriette whispered.

Anne walked between Henriette and Camille as they made their way to the *Salle de Buffet*. This was their first evening meal with Nicolas and Thomas, and Anne was as enthralled over the prospect as Henriette. Being in the same room with her patroness's grandson for an entire meal—knowing the stirring effect he had on her—had her on edge. She hadn't been able to forget the raw desire she'd seen in Nicolas's eyes before parting in the drawing room. Its seductive lure had incited a craving she couldn't vanquish.

"Really, Henriette, you are making much out of nothing." Camille's statement arrested Henriette's steps.

"Much out of nothing?" Henriette's eyes were wide with disbelief. "Dear sister, do the words"—she lowered her voice a notch—"'*Gilbert Leduc*' mean anything to you?"

Camille frowned. "Of course they do. They mean as much to me as they do to you, Anne, our dear Comtesse—not to mention all the women who have entrusted their stories to *him*."

"Then perhaps you can explain to me how we are to interview the very skittish Madame de Montbel and Madame de Boutette for Gilbert Leduc's next stories with these gentlemen here? You know the next volume must be brought to press in three weeks or Bruno won't print it. The more popular the books become, the more risk there is for those involved."

Camille frowned. "I'm quite aware of the deadline and the risks. What I don't understand is why you are fretting over the presence of Savignac and Gamory."

Henriette's mouth fell agape. She turned to Anne. "Will you please explain it to her?"

"Camille . . ." Anne strove for a more reasonable tone than Henriette's, though her sisters' bickering was grating on her patience. Like Henriette, she didn't relish having anyone whom she didn't know staying at the hôtel when one of Gilbert Leduc's volumes was in the works.

Especially a man as inflaming as Nicolas de Savignac.

"Leduc's identity must be protected at all cost," Anne said. "Especially since behind his pen are a number of women who have provided scathing secrets for Leduc's stories. There would be disastrous consequences for them if they were exposed."

"And the consequences for Leduc would be even worse," Henriette added for good measure.

"But these gentlemen are part of the Comtesse's family. Nicolas de Savignac is her very own grandson," Camille countered. "Surely that makes him trustworthy enough to—"

"To what? To tell him of Leduc?" Henriette sputtered. "*Are you mad?*"

Camille jabbed her fists into her waist. "I assure you I have complete command of my faculties. Henriette, you are—"

"Enough, please. Both of you," Anne demanded. Usually the one to settle her siblings' arguments, she was not in the mood for this tonight. "Camille,"—she turned to her younger sister—

"Madame de Cottineau is estranged from her grandson, and we don't know her reasons for it. Until she returns and we speak to her, we'll not reveal a thing to Savignac or Gamory. We'll not put anyone in jeopardy."

Henriette crossed her arms. "I don't trust Savignac."

"You haven't even met him yet," Camille said.

Anne had, and she didn't trust him either, or more particularly, herself around him, the physical calamity he inspired a serious detriment. And something she intended to get under control. Lest it got out of control. "We won't allow this situation to turn into a problem."

With resolve, Anne stalked toward the dining hall once more. Her sisters quickly fell into step. There was no other option, really. Leduc wrote the sorts of stories that needed to be written. Had to be told.

And would be published. On time.

After a few silent moments, Henriette conceded. "You're right, of course, Anne. Among the three of us, we can entertain our two guests until the Comtesse returns—and keep them from stumbling onto our secret. Isn't that right, Camille?"

"Yes, of course."

"Good. Then there is nothing left to argue about and nothing to be concerned over," Anne said, with more confidence than she felt. Why was she riddled with niggling doubts? What was the threat, really? "I doubt either gentleman has ever even heard of Leduc." Nicolas and Thomas came from the country, preferring to live at their country estates over Paris, as some nobles did. Leduc's popularity was for the most part contained inside the city. "And even if they know of him and his books, even if they see a few women come and go from the Comtesse's home over the next few days, they'd never conclude Leduc is under this roof." Anne glanced at each sister. "Right?"

"Right," they responded in chorus.

The tension in Anne's body eased the more she thought of the situation. Her biggest challenge in all this was to keep her distance from her patroness's enigmatic grandson.

And how difficult could that be?

With her sisters sharing the duties as hostess, she could limit her time in Nicolas's company—until she'd mastered her maddening reactions to him.

Anne's next book would go to press on time without their houseguests ever knowing that the notoriously famous author—who had tongues wagging in every Salon in the city—was right under their noses. Her books of poetry had never been as popular as her Gilbert Leduc volumes.

But she didn't write under the name "Gilbert Leduc" for the notoriety.

What motivated her pen were the women behind the stories—and their personal experiences that hit close to home and heart.

Before she knew it, Madame de Cottineau would return, deal with her grandson as she saw fit, and be delighted to find that Anne had published a new volume to titillate Leduc's readers.

She exchanged knowing smiles with her sisters. By the look in their eyes, she knew they were in accord; Leduc was a secret they wouldn't reveal.

Not to anyone outside their trusted circle.

There were many who'd tried to learn who was behind Leduc's pen. None had succeeded. No one ever would.

Keeping their secret from two men who weren't even interested in Leduc wasn't going to be difficult.

In fact, this was going to be easy.

CHAPTER THREE

Laughter rippled through the *Salle de Buffet*. The women were starting to relax. Nicolas was pleased as he chuckled along with his dining companions at the latest witty exchange.

Sweeping his gaze down the long elegant table, he glanced at each of the three sisters. Then at Thomas. Seated at opposite ends of the table, their gazes met and Nicolas could tell by his friend's expression that they were in agreement: the night was going well. Even the rather icy Henriette was beginning to offer a smile and the occasional laugh.

In short, Nicolas was making great progress; he was lowering the ladies' guards a charming comment at a time.

His eyes were drawn back to Anne. Repeatedly during the meal he'd caught himself watching her. Practically gawking at her. The candles on the silver torchères lined around the room cast an orange light, making the shade of her coppery curls bedazzling.

Making her skin look warm and so enticing.

He was dying to trail his fingers along the contour of her scooped neckline over the gentle swell of her breasts. He was dying to do far more than that with the enchanting poetess. Fantasies of her naked in his bed, wet with wanting, ran rampant in his mind.

Nicolas shifted in his chair, his stiff prick straining uncomfortably inside his breeches. *Merde*. She was seated to his right, dressed in a simple gown—hadn't done more than offer polite conversation—and she was driving him to distraction.

Anne brought a spoonful of soup to her lips.

By God, his yearning to possess that lush mouth mounted by the moment.

"Do tell us, Nicolas," Henriette's voice cut through his thoughts. "What has driven such a wedge between you and your grandmother? Why the estrangement?"

"Henriette!" Camille chastised.

Anne simply met his gaze and held it. By the look in her beautiful dark eyes, he could tell she was curious about the answer.

He decided to offer an honest one. "My mother married my father—a man my grandmother didn't care for. She disowned her when she learned of their secret marriage ceremony."

There was silence for a moment as the women absorbed his response.

"Why would the Comtesse object to your father as a husband for her daughter?" Anne asked softly. He liked her voice. He couldn't help but wonder at the sultry sounds she made in the throes of passion, what she'd sound like when she came. Or what the tight clasp of her wet sex around his thrusting cock would feel like . . .

She was staring at him. Waiting. Nicolas shot a glance at the others at the table. They all sported similar expectant expressions on their faces.

He cleared his throat. *Dieu, focus.* "Because my father was an ass, and he remained that way until his last breath." By the expression on her lovely face, it was obvious he'd surprised her with his bluntness. *Christ. That could have been put a little more gently.*

If he didn't bed her soon, he was going to lose his fucking mind.

"He—He didn't treat your mother well?" Camille voiced the question that was likely on everyone's mind.

"No, Camille, he did not." And despite her reservations, his coldhearted grandmother had never once inquired about her daughter's well-being—from the day she married until her death two years ago.

Camille lowered her head.

"Husbands seldom do—treat their wives well, that is," Anne said. "Your mother was not alone in that regard."

"Oh?" This was a direction he definitely wanted to go. Thanks to the forward Vignon sisters, they were making it easy for him. "And why do you say that?"

"Because it's the truth," Henriette interjected.

He dragged his eyes away from Anne. "Is it your truth, madame?"

She cocked a brow at him.

"Forgive me, but since we're being candid with each other, I thought you wouldn't mind my inquiring," Nicolas added.

Henriette set down her spoon. "I do mind—not about you asking questions, for we have nothing to hide here. But about discussing the subject of my late husband. He had a lot in common with your father, you see. He, too, was an ass."

Nicolas briefly glanced at Thomas.

Henriette rose. "If you will excuse me, I shall return to my chambers now. Good night."

Nicolas and Thomas were on their feet immediately. Henriette stalked out of the room.

Camille was the next to rise. "I should make certain she's all right."

With his eyes, Nicolas motioned Thomas to follow Camille out.

"Camille," Thomas called out, halting her steps. "Please, allow me to escort you." He offered his arm. Together they walked out of the *Salle de Buffet*.

Nicolas turned his attention to Anne. She was standing and he knew she was about to offer her excuses to leave.

"I have ruined the evening. I'm sorry. I didn't mean to cause distress." This was *not* how he'd intended the evening to end. Distracted by Anne, he'd blurted out his question to Henriette when he should have taken more care to ascertain the answer.

"Henriette will be fine. She is still sensitive about the late Baron and doesn't like to be questioned about him."

"I gather theirs was not a marriage filled with wedded bliss?"

She shook her head. "No, hardly that. Like your mother, my sister fell in love—and suffered for it."

He walked around the table and stopped before her. A light floral scent emanated from her beautiful hair, tantalizing his senses. "You sound as though you don't care for love."

From the moment he drew close, her cheeks took on a pretty blush, and Nicolas noted the rapid beating of her pulse along the side of her slender neck. Telltale signs of his heated effect on her.

These were exactly the reactions he wanted from her. And they were more than inciting his own carnal responses—her proximity causing his blood to flow faster. Making his cock feel harder and heavier than ever before.

She glanced at the door, and then at his mouth. Her desire was evident, but so was her unease at being alone with him. His greedy cock twitched. *Easy now.* If he moved too quickly, she'd bolt from the room. He'd already made mistakes tonight. He wouldn't make another. This mission was too important to him.

The matter required finesse. Patience. For the first time ever, he struggled with both—thanks to the bewitching writer with flame-colored hair.

"No, I don't believe in love," she stated firmly. He was disappointed in her answer, and he had no idea why he should be. He wasn't much of a believer in the fickle emotion either, but he'd read her works. They were filled with romantic sentiment. Romantic sentiment she'd clearly lost. Was it her sister's disagreeable marriage that had jaded her? Or Anne's own personal experience?

"But I'm told you write poetry. Love poems, to be precise."

"I do . . . rather . . . I did . . . two volumes of love poems . . . a while ago." Anne mentally cringed. She sounded like a babbling fool.

He was standing so close—too close—trapping her between the table and his tall sculpted form. From the moment she'd walked into the room and saw him standing in the dining hall with Thomas, her blood had warmed. Now it raced through her veins white-hot.

If he'd step back, she could think. As it was, it took every effort just to keep her breathing even, so that she didn't humiliate herself by panting in heat. How in heaven's name did she end up alone with him? This wasn't supposed to happen. Her sisters weren't supposed to abandon her in his company, but then, they had no idea how he ignited her senses.

"What do you write now?" he asked, his voice low. It reverberated inside her, making the ache between her legs grow fiercer. The very ache that had started from the moment he'd escorted her to her chair and then sat so near. She resented the way he was affecting her—worse—that she couldn't curb her responses to him. He was a nobleman. She didn't trust his kind, preferring poets and dramatists. She knew what the upper class were capable of, and yet, he'd still managed to sweep into the Comtesse's home, and awaken her long-dormant body with no effort at all.

"I . . . I'm working on . . .volumes...various ones." Another imbecilic response.

He tilted his head slightly to one side. "Volumes of what?"

"They are stories of intrigue and adventure." She didn't lie well when the most disarming pair of gray eyes was on her. Well, actually it wasn't a complete lie. Gilbert Leduc's stories did have intrigue, and getting the volumes published was an adventurous venture, to say the least.

A slight smile teased his lips. "Adventure?" He dipped his head, bringing his most kissable mouth closer to hers. *"Excitement . . ."* His warm breath caressed her lips. "That appeals to you, does it?"

Not this kind of excitement. *This* kind of excitement could only lead to trouble and heartache. And at the moment, she'd rather not be quite as *excited* as she felt.

Uncharacteristic thoughts of what that mouth would feel like against her skin were rushing through her mind.

"I should go." Now. Quickly. Before she did something foolish.

He didn't move. Instead, his light gray eyes held her gaze, then moved to her mouth, and for a moment she thought he might . . . would he . . . *kiss her?*

Her heart pounded. She held her breath. Waiting. Anticipating. Frozen with expectation.

His gaze met hers once more, and after a long drawn-out moment, he took a step back. "Good night, Anne."

She let out a breath and tamped down the disappointment that surged inside her.

"Yes. Good night."

Her heart still thundering, her limbs shaky, she stepped around him and proceeded toward the door.

"Wait." He caught her hand, surprising her.

He stepped closer and gently brushed a lock of her hair from her cheek. The light caress sent a rush of liquid heat from her core. What was it about this man that made her react this way? She was shamelessly vulnerable to him in a way she'd never been with any man.

Not even Roland.

"Anne, I hope I can count on your help," he said softly.

"Help?"

"With my grandmother. You know her better than I do. I want to learn everything I can about her. I need your help to do that. I want to understand her mind. Her heart. If you don't help me, I fear I'll fail in my attempt to forge a relationship with her. My mother went to her grave never having reconciled with the Comtesse. She isn't getting any younger. This may be my only opportunity to form a bond between us."

Anne forced a polite smile, her insides still in a frenzy. "My sisters and I will do what we can, but I can't promise results."

"I doubt Henriette will want to have much to do with me after tonight, and Camille seems far more interested in spending time with Thomas. You're the only one who can help me. Please, say you will." His expression was beseeching.

If her thoughts hadn't been so heated, she might have chosen her next words carefully. Instead, she said, "Well . . . I suppose–"

"Excellent!" Nicolas pressed a kiss to her hand, his mouth lingering a second or two longer than necessary. His warm lips against her skin felt sublime. A hot tremor shivered through her. "You can begin enlightening me on everything I should know about the Comtesse tomorrow." He flashed her a bedeviling smile, then turned on his heel and left the room.

Oh, God . . .

CHAPTER FOUR

Nicolas clenched his jaw. Thomas stood near the hearth—one hand on the mantel and the other clutching his side—laughing, the irritating sound reverberating in Nicolas's chambers.

"Let me see if I have this right . . ." Thomas said, fighting back a snicker. "You manage to get the comely Anne de Vignon alone, and though there is mutual physical attraction between you, and you could tell she wanted—*hungered*," he emphasized theatrically, "for a kiss, you denied her, and purposely left her wanting more."

Nicolas crossed his arms and sat back in his chair. "There is nothing wrong with that approach," he responded tightly over Thomas's new bout of laughter.

Thomas sobered up enough to say, "But wait, that's not all. Then, you—*le Loup*—a man with a reputation for being irresistible to the finer sex and having uncanny shrewdness in all situations—cleverly cornered her into helping you forge a relationship with your grandmother, which would, of course, give you an excuse to be in her company . . ." Thomas was laughing again, unable to continue.

Nicolas uncrossed his arms and rose. "What is wrong with that? It was a solid tactic to take."

Sobering, yet still chuckling, Thomas walked over to the small side table. "Yes, and for the first time since I've known you, my friend, *le Loup* miscalculated. While you were convinced she would be spending endless hours acquainting you with facts about the Comtesse, offering up promiscuous pleasures, and divulging information about Leduc, your 'solid' tactic got you this instead." He swiped up the note.

Nicolas,

I know how much you want to get to know your grandmother. I have thought of how best to help you with the Comtesse and what I could offer that would aid you in that regard. After much consideration, I believe I know just what you require.

Sincerely,
Anne

Thomas gestured toward the open trunk that accompanied the note. "Stacks of old dusty books." Thomas pulled one out, held it up and wiggled his brows. "All your grandmother's favorites." He laughed. "Not nearly as good as a tumble and a confession, but you might discover that you and your grandmother have some common literary preferences." Thomas roared.

Nicolas approached Thomas and snatched the note from his hand. "I'm glad you find this amusing. Perhaps you've forgotten that we are doing all this on behalf of the King." He stalked to the window and stared down at the courtyard below, clutching the note in his fist.

He'd thought he had her eating out of the palm of his hand.

It had taken enormous will not to kiss her when she'd looked at him so expectantly last eve. He'd left the room burning for her, certain that he'd be rewarded for his efforts with her company today. Not to mention her heightened desire.

Instead he got a trunk full of books.

He cared not what his grandmother read, nor to learn any more about her. What he already knew was more than enough. He needed to spend time with Anne. Alone. He needed to sate the untamable hunger he had for her. Clearly, it was beginning to seriously cloud his judgment. She was occupying his waking thoughts and, last night, his erotic dreams.

As soon as he'd received the books and the note, he'd gone to find Anne. Even went so far as to go to her private rooms, but was stopped by the somber servant, Vincent, who informed him that the Comtesse never allowed anyone to disturb the sisters when they were sequestered in their rooms writing.

"Oh, come now, Nicolas. Allow me to enjoy your misstep. You make so few." Thomas pulled another book from the trunk. "Are you going to read any of these?"

"Put the damned books down. What success have you had?" he snapped. "Have you obtained any information from Camille?"

Thomas tossed the books back in the trunk. "As a matter of fact, I have. She told me about Henriette's late husband, the penniless Baron de Pierpont, who squandered what little money they had on drinking, cards and debauchery. A '*cruel man, especially when into his cups,*' she'd said. And when Henriette miscarried the one and only time she was with child, the Baron refused to return home and sent her a scathing note telling her she couldn't do anything right. Not even give him an heir. I think Henriette is Gilbert Leduc. She's definitely still bitter about her husband."

"We need proof," Nicolas said. "Something undeniable and damning." Since Anne was indisposed, he was going to use his time to search the hôtel for evidence.

He wasn't finished with the pretty poetess. She wanted him. Felt the carnal hunger between them, whether she wished to admit it or not. She was playing a cat and mouse game.

Well, he never backed away from a challenge. Nor would he botch this crucial mission—his very first for the King.

She couldn't hide in her chambers forever.

When she came out, he'd be waiting.

*****

Madame de Montbel blew her nose loudly into her lace handkerchief.

"What he's done is cruel, I tell you," she cried. Tears dampened her rounded cheeks, her face mostly crease-free, despite her advancing years. "His misdeeds must be exposed as only Monsieur Leduc's stories can do—God bless the man."

Seated at her desk in her antechamber, Anne dipped her quill into the crystal inkwell, ready to take notes. "Yes, of course. He'll do his best," she said, compassion in her tone.

She always did her best for the women who came looking for some measure of satisfaction, their woes ranging from moderate to severe.

The men in their lives the root cause.

As master of the household, a man had absolute authority. His actions were above reproach. Uncontestable. It mattered little to him or his male peers if those very actions caused a woman humiliation. Hardship. Heartbreak. Expected to endure it, a woman was without recourse of any kind.

Until Gilbert Leduc came along.

Born of Anne's imagination for just this purpose, Leduc offered women an opportunity to tell their stories. And exact some revenge.

Each and every story was laced with a healthy dose of scandalous yet factual detail about the men in her tales.

The titillating tidbits were what made Anne's stories—*Gilbert Leduc's stories*—wildly popular. And what incensed the men. The angrier they got, the more it pleased the women she wrote for. These men deserved the public scrutiny, and at times, the ridicule. Not to mention the frustration of not knowing who Leduc was or where he got his information from.

It gave Anne great pride to know that the precautions she'd put in place had successfully kept anyone from learning Leduc's identity. The information that made its way into the stories was carefully chosen, so that it never gave away the woman offering up the details.

Madame de Montbel wiped her tears and leaned closer. "Have you ever met Gilbert Leduc?"

"No, madame. He's very strict about maintaining his anonymity. We simply take notes for him. The notes are dropped off in various secret locations around the city—and the locations always change. I have no idea who the man is." That was the usual answer she gave.

Together with the Comtesse, Anne chose the women Leduc wrote about; her patroness knew who could be trusted to come to her home and provide details for Gilbert Leduc's stories. And despite the cautious selection, none was told Gilbert Leduc and Anne were one and the same.

"Of course. He must be careful not to be exposed. I understand," Madame de Montbel said. "Now, where was I? Ah, yes, my son-in-law, the Duc de Falloux, asked for a *Lettre de Cachet* to be drawn up against my dear daughter two months ago, forcing her into confinement at a cloister. She isn't free to leave. Nor is she allowed visitors. Including me and her own children! He forbids it. Her imprisonment there could be indefinite." She sobbed then blew her nose again.

Sadly, Anne had heard stories like these before. A man could have orders drawn up against his "unmanageable" wife or other female members of his family, and have them confined to a prison or convent, or in some cases, even exiled. Without trial. Sometimes with little or no provocation. It was an abuse of power.

"What is his reason for having her cloistered?" Anne asked. Not that he really needed one.

"He doesn't approve of his wife having friends. In particular, Madame de Santerre."

Anne wasn't surprised.

Madame de Santerre was an educated intelligent woman and a darling of the more prestigious Salons. A young widow, she was independent and witty, with a sharp mind and an impressive knowledge of literature.

"He said that Madame de Santerre wasn't fit company, that she was too high-spirited for his 'feebleminded, impressionable' wife. That's what he called *my* Eléonore," she scoffed, disgusted.

What nonsense. More like, the man was afraid his wife might develop opinions of her own, like Madame de Santerre. Or perhaps he was simply looking for an excuse and wanted the Duchesse out of the way.

Keeping her comments to herself, Anne diligently recorded Madame de Montbel's statements. Dipping her quill back into the inkwell, she said, "Go on."

"When he caught Eléonore with books given to her by Madame de Santerre, he had her tossed into the cloister. He felt she'd been corrupted and needed to spend some time in religious devotion *'to reflect on her behavior,'* he'd said. He, on the other hand, immediately moved his favorite paramour into the hôtel—under the same roof as my grandchildren—and carries on openly, making no attempt to be discreet at all. Can you believe that?"

She could indeed. Men thought nothing of the hypocrisy of it all. A man could easily see a woman's actions as corrupt but never recognize his own wrongdoings.

Madame de Montel shook her head and dried more tears, clearly heartbroken. Anne wanted to offer consolatory words, but what could she say to diminish the woman's misery?

Setting a blue velvet purse down on the desk, Madame de Montel said, "This is compensation for Monsieur Leduc's trouble."

Anne pushed the purse back. "He accepts no payment from those who provide him with stories, madame. Your satisfaction with the work is compensation enough for him."

"Then please provide him with a note expressing my thanks and stress to him that I want him to show, through his pen portrait and story, just what kind of scoundrel the Duc is. He's to spare him no mercy." No longer did Madame de Montel weep. Her expression was hard, her eyes now narrowed.

"Of course," Anne assured.

"And now to address that aspect of the story that Leduc's readers love—that scandalous morsel they all devour." For the first time since Madame had been escorted to Anne's private apartments, she formed a smile, a bit of joy entering her eyes. "There is something I have learned about the Duc that I'm certain he wouldn't want others to know. He dares to question my daughter's character. Well, I have a bit of information to expose that will have everyone questioning his."

Uncertain what she was about to hear, Anne waited, quill inked and ready. There was nothing anyone could do to have Eléonore de Falloux freed. Or reunited with her children. Gilbert Leduc was not about to right a wrong here, but he was going to make sure that the Duc's callous actions didn't go unpunished.

*****

Nicolas ran his fingertips along the top shelving in the library, his arm stretched high. Methodically moving around the perimeter of the room, row by row, he glided his fingers over the smooth wood, until he'd checked them all.

No key.

Frustrated, he glanced across the room at the locked desk near the windows.

He'd already searched his grandmother's chambers. There, too, he'd located a writing desk.

Also locked.

He'd looked under the furniture and in every nook and cranny where a key could be hidden in his grandmother's rooms, and had stopped the search only when it was clear the key wasn't in her private apartments.

And—*merde*—he wasn't having any more success here in the library than he'd had upstairs.

With Henriette, Anne and Camille in their respective rooms, their private apartments couldn't be searched. Nicolas had hoped instead that a search of the Comtesse's desks would yield the evidence needed to prove Henriette was Gilbert Leduc.

Nicolas raked a hand through his hair. One master key could very well open both desks. If hidden in the library, it was possible the key was between the pages of one of the thousands of books lining the floor-to-ceiling shelves.

How was he ever going to locate something so small in such a vast collection of volumes? He didn't want to resort to trying to pick the lock, but would if he didn't find the key. Soon.

One of the volumes near the door caught his eye. Nicolas pulled it off the shelf. A slight smile tugged at the corner of his mouth as he gazed at the title. He'd read this book.

A book of poetry written by an alluring woman with the most magnificent red hair.

Anne de Vignon.

A hot rush streaked through him. He was anxious to see her, more than he could ever comfortably admit, and wondered how much longer she'd be sequestered in her rooms.

This time there'd be no holding back. This time he was going to give her what she'd been begging for with her eyes last night.

Nicolas opened the book and thumbed through it. He'd enjoyed Anne's poems. Her romantic verses at times were moving. He found himself—to his astonishment—lost in its pages.

He could only imagine the amusement Thomas would derive from *that*.

Nicolas turned back to the first page, where it indicated that the book had been printed in Paris and—more important—that it had passed the Royal Censor and had received permission to be published.

The book was completely legal.

Unlike Gilbert Leduc's books.

Nicolas had to give Henriette credit. She'd cleverly twisted the law to her benefit. Leduc's books claimed to be printed by a foreign publisher—which made them legal for purchase in France.

Foreign books didn't need royal consent the way domestic books did.

But the claim was false. The volumes weren't being printed out of the country by a foreign publisher. They were *not* foreign at all. Acting on a suspicion he'd had from the beginning, Nicolas had tracked down the press printing Leduc's books—located right in Paris.

In short, it wasn't just the sensational subject matter that made the books a problem. The entire illegal operation—from author to printer—would have to be brought to the attention of the King.

Nicolas heard fast footsteps approaching the room. He jerked his head up, froze, and listened.

Anne swept into the library and stalked straight to the desk. Instinctively, Nicolas slipped behind the nearby door. There was a brown ledger in her hand.

Setting the ledger on the desk, Anne pulled at the gold chain around her neck. A locket slid out of her bodice. She opened it, took out a key, and unlocked one of the desk drawers. Putting the ledger inside the desk, she relocked it, placing the key back in the locket.

Transfixed, Nicolas watched as the gold pendant slid down her smooth skin into her bodice once more.

Now there's a hiding place worth exploring.

Nestled between her soft breasts was the very item he needed. The very item he intended to get his hands on. He was about to have the key and the beautiful author. He liked this mission more and more with each passing day.

Nicolas stepped out from behind the door, hiding his smile.

Anne looked up and started. *"Nicolas . . ."* she breathed. The breathless way she'd uttered his name made his heart hammer and his sac tighten.

Clearly, she hadn't expected to see him. It confirmed for him—just as he'd surmised—that she'd sent the trunk of books to his chambers for reasons other than to better acquaint him with his grandmother. She was trying to keep him busy—a clever parry on her part. She was attempting to elude him. Moreover, she was trying to avoid the sexual lure between them.

There was no way he was going to let her.

Nicolas stopped before the desk. His cock was already stiffened and eager. "I've startled you."

"No . . . well, yes. I thought . . ." She was adorably flustered. She wasn't a giddy woman. She was educated, intelligent and always poised, and he loved that he could fluster her. However, that she caused him to make missteps was something he didn't find quite as appealing.

"Rather . . . I didn't see you there." She bit her lip.

Oh, how he was going feast on that pretty mouth. In fact, on her entire sweet, edible form until he got his fill.

Before she left this room again, she was going to express, not avoid, her desire for him.

"Was that your intrigue and adventure story you placed in the desk?" Nicolas kept his tone light, feigning mild interest.

"No. It was simply an accounting ledger. Henriette often helps your grandmother with accounting matters. I was placing it there for her."

"I see." He would see—the ledger and the rest of the contents of the desk. Later. After he had the key. And the woman before him. "It was very kind of you to send the trunk of books. Thank you," he said.

She formed a smile, donning a cordial mask. One he wanted stripped away. Her writings had given him a glimpse of the real Anne de Vignon. Definitely passionate. He wanted to see more. Know more.

Sample some of that very passion firsthand.

"You're welcome. I hope you enjoy them as much as the Comtesse. You may discover you have more in common with her than you think."

Jésus-Christ, he hoped not. "Perhaps so. But I noticed that some books were missing. Ones I'm sure she loves."

Her delicate brows drew together. "Oh?"

He held up the book still in his hand. "Like this one."

Anne pulled her gaze away from his handsome face to the brown leather volume. Her book of poems.

"This is yours, isn't it?" he asked.

"Yes."

In his dark blue justacorps and breeches, he looked so good. So tall and strong. So potently male. Was it possible that he looked even more beautiful today?

"Why didn't you add this to the trunk? Surely the Comtesse loves your work," he said. "I doubt she'd be your patroness otherwise."

Her two volumes of poetry had been written when she was a different person. With whimsical ideas of love. Before Roland had disillusioned and disenchanted her.

Both she and Henriette had had the misfortune of knowing love and its stinging effect.

"I didn't think you'd be interested in reading a book of love poems."

Something glinted in his eyes. "You're right. I'm not interested in reading a book of love poems." He sauntered around the desk. She watched his approach, heat flaring in her belly. He stopped beside her, his body all but touching hers, and handed her the book. "I'd like you to read it to me."

CHAPTER FIVE

Anne forced her gaze down to the book in her hands—a completely futile attempt to divert her attention and collect her wits. Maddeningly, she didn't have to look at Nicolas to know he was there. Every fiber of her being was acutely aware of him.

And what he was doing to her . . .

Her pulse raced. Her breasts felt achy, and her sex was slick. She was a mortifying mess. What irony—for a woman who wrote the stories she did. Who tried to embolden women and discourage this very sort of vulnerability.

With his exceptional looks and charismatic comportment, Nicolas was just the kind of man who could sweep a woman off her feet, into his bed. And shatter her heart.

She'd already been down that road.

She'd never venture there again.

And yet, as he stood close to her, all the warnings, all her good reasoning, were being drowned by the powerful urges flooding her body. He tempted her. Sorely.

She wasn't naïve. She knew he was trying to seduce her. From the moment they met, all the signs were there. It was in his every look, every well-timed touch and well-practiced tone. Other men had attempted to stir her desire with similar tactics, but none had invoked her interest. Until Nicolas.

She had no idea why this man called to her on such a carnal level. Especially since she'd been so dead inside for so long.

Nicolas moved behind her. She felt his unmistakable erection against her bottom. Briefly, she closed her eyes. The light pulsing between her legs had just turned into a hungry throb.

He slid his arms forward, brushing along the sides of her waist, and opened the book in her hands. Flipping a few pages, he then murmured against her ear, "Read this one."

He removed his arms but the sensations remained in the wake of his touch.

Anne scanned her verses, quickly realizing he'd selected one of the most provocative, amorously suggestive poems in the book. She'd forgotten just how passionate her words were. Emotional and physical yearnings were in every line.

She felt a twinge of sadness as she realized how much she'd changed, dismayed that she was revisiting old wounds—thanks to Nicolas. Her intuition told her he'd read some of her work and selected this very evocative poem intentionally. A purposeful strike at her pathetic weakened state. He might be a master of seduction, but she would not be played.

But you want this . . . She shoved the thought away, trying to mute her base needs.

It was time to put an end to this. She'd tried being polite. She'd tried keeping a distance. She'd even tried diverting his attention to keep him otherwise occupied by sending him his grandmother's books. All to no avail.

He might be her patroness's grandson but he was overstepping his bounds and she was going to rein him in.

Anne shut the book, tossed it onto the desk and spun around to face him. "I know what you're trying to do." Her tone was firm, yet her ire hadn't diminished her fever.

His face was unreadable, giving nothing away. "Oh? What am I trying to do?"

Jamming her fists into her hips, she rose onto the balls of her feet so that she was closer to eye level when she responded, "Bed me!"

One dark brow rose, then his lips twitched as he held back a smile. He leaned in so that his mouth was mere inches from hers.

"I know what you're trying to do, Anne. Avoid me." His warm breath made her lips tingle. "You're afraid."

She dropped back down onto her heels. "Afraid? Of you? You jest."

"No, not of me. Of you. You want me and it frightens you. Admit it."

She gave a mirthless laugh. "Good Lord, you are conceited."

A slow knee-weakening smile spread across his mouth. "No. Just observant. Your body betrays you," he said with far too much smugness.

She hated it that he was right. Her body was betraying her. This tormenting need and the moisture between her legs were the last things she wanted.

No, the last thing you want is for him to "know" that you desire him.

"If it's bed sport you seek, I suggest you look elsewhere. I am not looking for a lover." Her body railed at her words.

"Why not? Do you already have one?"

"That's none of your concern."

"I'll assume that means *no*." He shook his head. "I am amazed."

"At what?"

"That such a beautiful woman has a cold empty bed, and no one to fulfill the carnal yearnings her body craves"—her sex contracted, a fresh wave of arousal flooding through her— "especially when it is obvious that she's so naturally drawn to sexual pleasures. I've read some of your work, Anne," he said. "Those poems were written by a woman of passion."

"I told you, I wrote those poems a long time ago. I'm not the same woman."

"Yes, you are. Now that the mask of propriety has dropped, the real Anne de Vignon finally appears. Spirited and fiery—just as your writing suggests. At last I get to see the real you."

"And why do you care to *see the real me?*" No one had ever expressed such an interest. Certainly no man. And only after Roland had left had she finally seen that he didn't care to know her either. "Why would it matter to you who I am?"

He brushed a lock of her hair behind her ear. "I find you as intriguing as you are desirable."

"Really," she responded blandly, though her fever spiked at his touch. "Please spare me your flowery words." She'd heard enough of them from Roland to last three lifetimes. "You are wasting your efforts."

Anne turned to leave. He caught her wrist. She snapped her head around, ready to deliver up some hot words, when he stunned her into silence by pressing her palm to the bulge in his breeches. "You make me hard every time you walk into the room. I'm willing to admit how much I want you," he said, his voice low, intoxicating. Anne fought back the strong urge to tighten her fingers around him. Even through his breeches she could tell he was thick and lusciously large, bringing to sharp focus the void between her thighs aching to be filled, and that a very lonely bed was waiting for her upstairs. "I'm not wasting my efforts as long as the desire is mutual. Your nipples are hard, begging for attention. Your pulse is racing and you're wet for me, aren't you?"

Wet? She'd soaked her *caleçons*.

He grazed her palm up his length and squeezed her hand hard against him. She lost her breath.

"Why not give in to the sexual pull between us?" he asked, releasing his hold of her hand. "Neither of us can seem to tame it. A carnal encounter between us is inevitable."

Her body burned for him . . . Could she really do this? "You're my patroness's grandson." She knew she was grasping for reasons. Dear God, she was still grasping his erection after he'd taken his hand away.

She released him.

In a quick fluid motion he picked her up and set her bottom down on the desk. She gasped and grabbed his shoulders. His hips were now suddenly wedged between her spread thighs. "That is no deterrence. She has nothing to do with this. She doesn't own your body. You do. You're a grown woman, Anne.

It's your decision to make. It's just sex. Some shared physical pleasures."

He was right. Love was one thing. Physical pleasure quite another. Unfortunately, she hadn't been any more successful with sex than she'd been with love.

Nicolas could tell she wanted to surrender to him. She wanted to give in to the demands of her body and this stunning attraction between them that was only growing stronger by the moment. He was so close . . .

Her procrastination was killing him.

Slipping his hands around her, he gripped her soft derrière and pulled her up against his cock. A small sound escaped her throat the instant he'd come in contact with her sensitized clit. There were too many damn clothes between them. "Are you a virgin, Anne?" He could tell that her sexual experience was rather limited, but how limited, he didn't know. "It's all right if you are. I'll leave you intact until you say otherwise," he assured her. "There are still decadent delights we can enjoy." He dipped his head and brushed his lips against hers. "Say yes, and we'll begin right now."

The tip of his cock was wet with pre-come. His sac was tight. His body screamed for release. This woman had him so completely undone.

Her hands slid down from his shoulders and fisted his justacorps at his chest, still indecisive.

He ran his tongue along the seam of her mouth and lightly bit her bottom lip. "Say it, and I'll make it worth your while." Rolling his hips, he stroked his length along the soft folds of her sex, this time with enough pressure to make her moan for him—a long sultry sound. *Oh, yes. That's it.* Mentally, he willed her to acquiesce. "Say yes . . . Do it, Anne . . . and we can indulge in some mutual gratification," he added. *Seigneur Dieu*, he was practically begging.

He'd never begged anyone for anything.

She pulled back slightly. "Mutual gratification?" She was breathless and flushed. "That's . . ." She swallowed. "That's what men say, but . . . in truth . . . in the boudoir they take their pleasure. Then they take their leave."

Merde. What was Henriette filling her head with? "Not all men are the same. Some of us enjoy giving pleasure as well as receiving it. There's nothing sweeter than a woman's release." Those spine-melting ripples along his thrusting prick when a woman came were exquisite, and something he'd never forgo. "It is a heady rush—empowering—to have someone desperate for you. Desperate for what you can give."

His words hit their mark. He saw curiosity spark in her eyes. She was intrigued. Clearly, she liked the idea of feeling empowered. It occurred to him just then, *She doesn't want to feel vulnerable.*

It was a barrier for her—one he intended to knock down.

To that end, Nicolas yanked her up against him harder and said, "You have me desperate for you. For what you can give—yourself." It was no lie. "So desperate, in fact, that I've got to have your mouth right now."

He crushed her lips, unsure whether she was going to protest. His kiss was hard and hungry, wanting to be inside her more than he wanted his next breath. She parted her lips and pressed her soft form against him. His arousal spiked, hurling him into a feral state, like none he'd known before. Voracious, he drove his tongue into her mouth. She tasted so good. He needed more.

His practiced fingers pulled at the ties on her bodice, impatiently separating it and yanking down her clothing until at last he uncovered her breasts.

Nicolas broke the kiss, his breaths harsh and rapid. He devoured the vision before him. Her breasts weren't large or small, but perfect. His mouth watered.

The gold locket dangled between the soft tempting mounds. It was suddenly an annoying distraction. He didn't want to think about the key inside. Or his mission. Right now, all he wanted to concentrate on was showing her just how good sex could be, knowing instinctively from the first moment their gazes had met that any carnal encounter between them was sure to be hot and intense.

Nicolas pulled the locket off. She made a small sound in protest.

"Shhhh. It's all right," he soothed. "It's in the way."

Pressing his palm against the nape of her neck, he pulled her forward and kissed her again, slow and deep, dropping the locket with a *clunk* onto the desk, so that she knew it was nearby.

She returned his kiss, her hands still clutching the lapels of his knee-length coat. He cupped her breast and grazed his thumb over one hardened nipple. She shivered.

Nicolas pinched, then lightly pulled on the pretty pink tip. Breaking the kiss, she tipped her head back with a soft cry, her glorious red hair spilling over her shoulders.

Good God, she was so sensuous.

Hot urgency thundered through him. His sac was so full of come, he could barely stand it. "Anne . . ." His voice was gruff with desire.

She opened her eyes, her gaze deliciously heated.

"You want more, don't you?" He rolled her nipple between his fingers. She whimpered.

He rolled the pebbled tip a little harder and was instantly rewarded with a stronger mew. "You like that? You want more?" he repeated.

She trembled. "Yes . . ."

He released her nipple, pushed her onto her back, then pinned her wrists against the desk. She stared up at him, her sweet breasts rising and falling with each rapid breath. "Good, because I'm going to give you more."

He lowered his head and sucked her nipple into his hungry mouth.

Anne arched off the desk with a strangled cry, lost to the wet heat drawing on the sensitive tip, each luscious pull of his mouth making her writhe and her sex leak. She'd never known such keen sensations, such engulfing need.

She'd never known a man like Nicolas de Savignac. There were many reasons she shouldn't be doing what she was doing, but with each silky suck of his mouth, her reasons eluded her and she couldn't think of one. For once, she didn't want to think. She wanted to feel. Anne closed her eyes . . . And this felt so sublime.

He turned to her other breast, lavishing upon it the same wicked torment—teasing licks, hard sucks, and light bites. He had her squirming, moaning, panting, starved for more.

He was giving, not taking. Yet in giving, he was getting something in return—the pleasure of her pleasure. This was all so new. She'd never heard any man refer to sex the way he did. This was the kind of passion she'd imagined when she wrote those poems years ago. This was the kind of passion she had envisioned experiencing one day. This was the kind of passion she'd convinced herself she'd never know.

With a growl, he tore his mouth off her. Her eyes flew open, her breathing sharp and shallow.

Releasing her wrists, he yanked her skirts up, layer by layer, his handsome face etched with heated determination. Her heart pounded away the moments until she felt him untie her drawers and pull them off with a fierce tug.

He tossed them carelessly onto the chair behind him, bent her knees, and pressed them back toward her, opening her wet sex to his view. She was so far gone, she wasn't in the least bit embarrassed.

His light gray eyes met her gaze. The corner of his mouth lifted in a smile. "You look delicious. Good enough to eat." Her insides danced. "Have you ever had a man pleasure you with his mouth?" he asked.

She'd never had a man pleasure her. Period. Her carnal experience was limited to her encounters with Roland. They'd left her disappointed and dissatisfied. What Nicolas was doing to her was already more pleasure than she'd ever known.

Somehow, Anne summoned her voice. "No."

"Then it's time one did." There was such wicked promise in his eyes, her heart lost a beat. She tensed, bracing herself for the thrill of his touch.

He tightened his grip on her knees. "Relax. All you have to do is to enjoy it."

She nodded. "Good. Fine. *Hurry.*" She was dying. She doubted she would have objected to anything he wanted at the moment.

Amusement flickered in his eyes for an instant before they darkened with desire once more. "I'm going to savor you." He lowered his head between her legs.

The first stroke of his tongue tore a cry from her throat. He stopped; his hand flew off her knee and covered her mouth. "You have to be quiet," he said, tossing a quick glance at the door.

She nodded again, quivering from the inside out.

Gripping both her knees firmly once more, Nicolas lowered his hot mouth onto her needy flesh and groaned. She bit her lip and swallowed down her wail of pleasure.

His skillful tongue licked her along her dewy folds, stimulating every overwrought nerve ending along the way. He varied between soft licks and stronger strokes. She sobbed for more. Nothing in her life had ever felt this good. Her orgasm was building, fast and fierce.

His masterful sucks on her swollen bud sent her rushing to the precipice, but he stopped her from toppling into ecstasy every time by pulling away and lightly blowing cool air against her hot nub, holding her enthralled. Driving her wild.

"Nicolas," she said, his name a plea.

He thrust his tongue inside her. She jerked. He then began sucking her juices, besieging her body with deep suctioning sensations. She squeezed her eyes shut, each pull of his mouth edging her closer and closer to the release she was frantic for.

He pulled back.

Her eyes flew open, dazed and desperate. She was on the brink!

"You taste so good," he said and licked her essence off his lips. "You're going to come for me hard, aren't you?"

"Yes!" exploded from her lips. "*Please*, don't stop."

Releasing one of her knees, Nicolas slid two fingers inside her. She moaned at his possession.

His fingers glided in and out of her soaked sex. She was instantly lost in the rhythmic plunge and drag making her inner muscles clench and release, pushing her once more toward a shattering climax.

"That's it, Anne. I'm not going to stop. You're going to come for me, *now*."

He swooped in and sucked her clitoris into his mouth with such stunning force, she lurched with a strangled scream.

Ecstasy burst inside her. Anne stiffened and convulsed, her orgasm rocking her body, as spasms rippled through her core, along his thrusting fingers. He grunted sharply, his mouth still firmly latched onto her, unrelenting. Digging her nails into her knees, she rode out the muscle-melting sensations, the shuddering contractions, until the final one ebbed.

Boneless and shaky, she felt him lower her legs and let them dangle over the edge of the desk. Her gown was bunched at her waist, her lower body still exposed.

Nicolas swiped his mouth with the back of his hand, his eyes ablaze with his physical need. "We're not done," he assured her, his voice rough with desire. Already his hands were on the ties of his breeches and he started to open them.

She didn't want to be done.

Anne rose onto her elbows and was about to tell him how much she wanted to feel him inside her, and that she wanted to bring him to a voluptuous climax, just as he'd brought her, when she saw him freeze. His chin jerked up, his attention directed at the door.

It was then she heard it. *Footsteps.*

They were getting louder, closer.

Her stomach dropped. She sat up, twisted around and gasped. The door was ajar and had never been fully closed, much less locked.

Nicolas swore, each word a low snarl, laced with frustration and fury at the impending interruption. He raked both hands through his dark hair and let out a sharp breath. "We'll have to finish this later." He cupped her cheeks and gave her a quick hard kiss. "I may just kill whoever is about to walk through that door." He pulled her skirts down over her legs. "Dress. Quickly." He refastened his breeches.

Her heart thundered as her fumbling fingers went to work on her bodice.

Nicolas picked up books that had been knocked off the desk during their amorous encounter, straightening the area around them. She hadn't realized they'd made such a mess.

The footsteps continued to approach at a strong and steady pace.

Finishing with her bodice, Anne slipped off the desk and onto her shaky legs, then smoothed her hair and her skirts, and checked her bodice again, making certain everything was secure.

Nicolas pulled her *caleçons* off the chair and stuffed them into the sleeve of his justacorps. He winked at her.

She felt her cheeks warm. "How do I look?" she asked.

He stepped closer. In her ear he whispered, "Like a woman who thoroughly enjoyed some carnal pleasures." She heard the smile in his voice.

Heat crept down from her face to her chest. He stepped back. "Don't forget this." Dangling from his finger was her gold locket.

"Thank you." She quickly slipped it on and tucked the pendant into her bodice.

Nicolas dropped down onto the settee, opened one of the books he'd picked up, and was thumbing through it casually when Henriette pushed the door open and swept into the room.

She stopped, glanced at Nicolas and cocked a brow at Anne. Anne managed the semblance of a smile.

"A wonderful poem, Anne," Nicolas said. "I enjoyed it very much." He flipped more pages. "Ah, and this one, 'One Spring Night'—absolutely lovely."

Henriette cleared her throat.

Nicolas twisted around. "Oh, Henriette . . ." He smiled and rose, looking as innocent as a babe. "Good day to you."

"Good day, Nicolas." Henriette walked over to the desk.

Anne didn't miss that Nicolas held the book strategically before him, covering his tented breeches. Nicolas met her gaze. His smoldering look weakened her knees. Outwardly, he put on a cool and polished performance. But on the inside, he burned for her.

Henriette pulled her locket out of her bodice and removed the key inside. "I see you are reading Anne's poetry," she said as she unlocked the desk drawer.

"Yes, and enjoying it very much. Knowing how much I want to get to know my grandmother, Anne graciously gave me a number of the Comtesse's favorite books. I'm looking forward to reading yours, too, Henriette."

"Really? Do tell me what you think of them." Her sister pulled the ledger out of the desk, then relocked it.

"Of course. I anticipate being enthralled." Nicolas gave a slight bow.

Dear God, the man was flawless and unflappable. Anne admired him for it, and yet, it was disquieting.

"Are you going to work here, Henriette?" she asked. "I was about to leave—"

"No, I'll take this to my rooms. If you are through, I'd like you to join me." Henriette walked toward the doors. "Until this evening, Nicolas."

"Until this evening, Henriette," he concurred, his tone and expression genial.

Henriette stopped at the doors. "Aren't you coming?" she asked Anne.

"I'll be along shortly." Anne waited until her sister left the library and her steps had receded before she approached

Nicolas. "You are too good." Her tone was light but her words were weighted.

A grin formed on his face. "Oh? And what specifically am I 'too good' at?"

He was hunting for a compliment, the cheeky devil. But then again, a man with his sexual skills had a certain right to be smug. "Your carnal skills notwithstanding, I was referring to your comportment. In fact, your comportment always."

He lifted a brow. "What about my comportment?"

"It is always polished. You give nothing away."

"I'm afraid I don't understand. Did you want me to give away what we did on the desk your sister was just using?"

"No, of course not. It's just . . ." She shook her head. "Forget it. It's nothing."

He frowned, tossed the book down onto the settee, then cradled her cheek in his palm. "What is it? Tell me."

She looked up into his face. "I've noted that men who are too polished, are too often . . . deceitful." She moved in closer. "I want you to be honest with me, Nicolas. Always."

"What just happened between us was honest. My desire for you is genuine. My desire to spend more such blissful moments with you is sincere."

Anne smiled. "I know. I enjoyed what we did. Very much." She grasped hold of his labels, rose onto the balls of her feet and brushed her mouth along the side of his neck, stopping at his pulse to draw lightly on his skin. His heart rate instantly increased beneath her lips. He groaned, his reactions to her an inebriating rush.

She craved his surrender. To turn the tables and bring him to his release, have him completely unravel for *her*. The notion was thrilling. It *was* empowering. And too tempting to walk away from, despite the niggling warnings in her head.

She couldn't wait to decimate his defenses. To peel back the layers and discover the real Nicolas. And she intended to do it, one caress and kiss at a time.

"Tonight, it is my turn to pleasure you," she murmured in his ear. "I want you inside me."

CHAPTER SIX

The moment Anne left, Nicolas slumped against the bookshelves and scrubbed a hand over his face.

Merde. His unsated body was in torment. Agony, actually, thanks to her heated words, her soft hot mouth.

She'd unbalanced him in the worst way.

His every impulse was to race after her, take her to her rooms and finish what they'd started. But he wouldn't do it no matter how powerful the urge. Not until he'd collected himself and was back in control.

Lifting his left hand, he opened his palm. A shiny gold key stared back at him, taken from the locket just before he'd handed it back to her.

It was a victory, but it felt like an empty one. He had the key. But not the woman. And he wanted her too damned much. Her taste was still on his tongue. She tasted sweeter than any female he'd ever had. Sampling her had only stoked the fire. Having to wait several hours before he could be with her was torture in the extreme.

Nicolas clenched the key tightly. At a full cock stand, his muscles taut, he shoved himself off the bookshelves and began to pace.

She was insightful. A little too intuitive. And as ludicrous as it was, her comment about deceitful men actually bothered him. Nicolas silenced the foreign emotion that was gnawing at him.

He was *not* deceitful. He was on a mission. There was a difference. He had a duty—and he was *not* going to feel guilty about it. If physical intimacies brought him closer to the truth, all the better. Especially when those ardent encounters were as fine as the one he'd just had.

There'd be no deviation from his initial plan. Anne was going to unwittingly aid him in solving the mystery of Leduc and gain him recognition in the Guard. Being a Musketeer was everything to him. Commanding the Musketeers was his long-held dream.

So why don't you check the desk? You've got the key.

Nicolas stopped dead in his tracks and dragged his gaze to it. Ebony and with gold inlay, it was an ornate piece of furniture.

And where you brought a beautiful author to a shattering release.

Thanks to their decadent diversion, now he knew for certain she wasn't a virgin. She'd had another lover, possibly more than one—though she wasn't overly experienced.

Who were they? How did they treat her?

The comment she'd made about men taking their pleasure and then their leave was also eating at him. He'd initially thought Henriette had put the notion in her head.

But now, he wasn't so certain . . .

Nicolas pulled out her *caleçons* from his jacket. Her scent swirled around him; his prick throbbed. He shoved the garment back in his justacorps.

So she'd made a negative comment or two about men. So what? Just because she'd made such statements, and just because she'd had some amorous experience, didn't prove she was Leduc.

Henriette was Leduc.

There is only one way to be certain . . .

His attention was drawn back to the desk. With a muttered oath, he marched over to it and sat down. Unlocking the first drawer, he began his search, trying to ignore the trepidation he felt.

His heart rate settled into slow hard thuds as he sifted through the content of each drawer, reading every letter and note he found. His grandmother's letters. Mostly from old friends. Meaningless to him.

Nicolas closed the third drawer and opened the final one. A yellow satin box was all it contained. Frowning, he pulled it out and untied the matching ribbon around the box and pulled off the lid.

More letters.

Only these were different. These ensnared him. These were addressed to his mother.

Nicolas flipped through them. At least twenty letters, all written by a grandmother he'd never known to a mother who'd regretted her marriage—yet was never forgiven for her impetuous act.

Scanning each letter, he was astonished to read remorse in the old woman's words. Cold anger slowly seeped through his body and congealed in his blood. Damn her. Why bother writing letters she never intended to send? *Merde.* What was the point? Was this some twisted way of purging her conscience? Having never sent the letters out clearly showed the Comtesse had chosen her pride over her daughter.

Now that his mother was gone, it was too late. The Comtesse would never have the opportunity to express her regrets.

Nicolas tossed the letters back in the box, disgusted. Yet at the same time he was . . . *relieved.* There was nothing damning Anne.

There is nothing that proves Henriette is Leduc either.

Now that he had the master key, he could search for proof—in the Comtesse's private rooms as well as Henriette's chambers.

Dismayed that he was feeling reluctant at hunting for evidence, he steeled his resolve, retied the yellow ribbon around the box, and locked it in the desk once again.

The key firmly clenched in hand, Nicolas stalked from the room with purposeful strides.

The King expected results. As did his Captain. He had a job to do. He'd get it done.

And in the meantime, none would be the wiser.

*****

Anne slammed her book of poetry shut. "I've decided to take a lover," she blurted out.

Camille gasped.

Sitting behind the desk, her quill frozen in hand, Henriette's mouth fell agape.

With a squeal, Camille jumped out of her chair and clapped her hands, the book on her lap falling to the floor. She rushed over and dropped down beside Anne on the settee.

"Who is it?" she asked with breathless anticipation. "It's Nicolas, isn't it? His eyes devour you whenever he looks at you." A giggle bubbled out of her.

Her younger sister's giddiness made Anne smile. "Yes, as a matter of fact, it is."

Slowly Henriette set the quill down, rose from the desk in Anne's private apartments, and walked around it, staring at Anne as if she just sprouted a horn out of the middle of her forehead, her expression a mixture of shock and horror. "Have you lost your mind?"

"No."

Camille let out another squeal of jubilation. "I think it's wonderful!"

Henriette glared at Camille, the same incredulous expression etched on her face. "Pray tell, what is wonderful about Anne and the Comtesse's grandson?"

"Well, Henriette," Camille began, "unless you're completely blind, you may have noticed he's incredibly handsome." Turning to Anne, she beamed once more. "And he's interested in our sister!"

Henriette rolled her eyes. "Good Lord." She approached and sat down in a nearby chair. The latest chapter of Gilbert Leduc's story that she'd been editing now lay forgotten on the desk. "He has beguiled you." Henriette shook her head. "I knew I didn't trust him."

"He has *not* beguiled her. Anne knows what she is doing," Camille defended. "Go ahead, Anne. Tell Henriette she's wrong."

"Perhaps I wish to be beguiled," Anne stated.

Henriette's eyes widened. "But he's only looking for a tumble."

"As am I." Anne's answer set Camille into a fit of laughter.

"You see! I told you, Anne knows what she's doing," Camille countered, then leaned into Anne. "Has Nicolas said or done anything to initiate a physical involvement? I must say, I've been having rather shameless thoughts about Thomas and wondering if he would—"

Henriette threw up her hands. "Am I the only one who has any good sense left? Anne, you are talking about the Comtesse's very own grandson. What will she say?"

"The Comtesse is no prude," Anne said.

"I think the Comtesse will not mind at all. She adores Anne, and she'll adore her grandson, once she gets to know him. He's very charming." Camille patted Anne's hand. "However, I do think you should still be discreet."

"Anne, I think this is a mistake." Worry creased Henriette's brow. "Though it pains me to mention it, you and I have hardly had good luck in selecting men. I married out of love . . . and look how disastrously that turned out. And then there's your involvement with Roland d'Orsay. He took your innocence and your heart before he left and married the Baron de Grimaud's daughter."

Anne leaned forward and squeezed her older sibling's hand. "Henriette, this is not about love. That is not what I am looking for." She'd found a man who stirred her. Excited her. She wanted more of the same. More of the wild abandon she'd experienced with Nicolas earlier.

He was nothing like Roland.

The sumptuous memory of what had happened in the library with Nicolas flooded her mind. Hot need instantly unfurled in her belly, sending waves of heat shimmering over her nerve endings. Her body tightened and ached for more.

Anne picked her book of love poems off her lap and held it up. "Do you see this, Henriette? Today, for the first time in a very long while, I reread my poetry." It had been jarring and revealing. "I realized just how withdrawn I've become. I used to want passion. After Roland, I wanted *nothing*. No passion of any kind—involving either the heart or the body. And this is how I have remained. Embracing nothing. It is empty."

She'd *gladly* turn her back on love, but in no way did she want to withhold herself from the glorious passion she'd discovered in Nicolas's arms.

With one wickedly delicious act, he'd showed her that she wasn't as dead inside as she thought. Moreover, he'd made her see the physical act of love in a whole new light. It wasn't simply an act where the man took and the woman gave. At least not with him.

Henriette frowned. "Your life is not empty. You are Gilbert Leduc. You are doing something with your writing. You are giving women a chance to speak through his stories."

"Yes, and I must confess that there are times during the interviews I feel like screaming, *'Is there not one decent man anywhere in the realm worthy of a woman's heart or body?'*" Anne let out a sharp breath and placed her book back down on her lap.

"What are you saying?" Henriette asked. "You can't be thinking of quitting—of no longer writing Leduc's stories. We couldn't earn enough to feed ourselves from our writing before. And you know how the Comtesse feels about Leduc's books."

"What I am saying is that we live in the most powerful nation in all of Christendom. A nation of twenty million people, half of which are men and none of which seem to have any appeal," Anne said.

Her sisters fell silent.

"Well, I have found one who appeals to me," she continued. "One can indulge in physical intimacies, share some bliss, without involving the heart. Men do it all the time. Why can't I?"

Her sisters looked at her with a mixture of emotions. The predominant one—concern.

Anne rose and helped Henriette up out of her chair. Guiding her back to the desk, she said, "Everything is fine and is going to remain that way. For me and for Leduc. His stories will continue to delight his avid readership. Now get back to editing so this story can be published."

She would never stop writing Leduc's stories. She believed in them. The Comtesse believed in them, and Leduc's readers clamored for them.

She'd never allow anything to interfere with them. Not even a heavenly affair with a beautiful man. The deadline approached. The volume had to be sent to the printer soon.

She had a job to do. She'd get it done.

And no one would be the wiser.

*****

Nicolas pressed the key into Thomas's palm. "Take this. It's the master key to the desks in the hôtel."

The afternoon had trickled by. At last it was evening. Only a few more hours before he'd be with Anne. *"I want you inside me."* Each time her provocative words entered his mind, it spiraled through his system, making his fever for her spike.

Thomas's eyes widened. "Where did you get it?"

"Anne." His response was purposely short and tight.

Thomas grinned. "I take it the lady's unaware you have her key?"

"That's correct."

Still grinning. "Care to share some details?"

"Absolutely. You have a stomach ailment," Nicolas said, taking the justacorps Thomas was about to put on and tossing the knee-length jacket onto a nearby chair in Thomas's rooms. "You're in great discomfort and are unable to go to supper."

"I am?"

"Yes, and I will offer your regrets to the ladies."

"Why can't I go to supper?"

"Because you're going to be searching Henriette's and Camille's private desks in their chambers. During the day and at night, a search is impossible. They are almost always in their rooms. The only time one can be conducted is while they're together in the *Salle de Buffet* for supper. I've already searched both of the Comtesse's desks. Neither desk yielded any evidence of any kind. I found nothing that proved or remotely hinted at the identity of the author of the pen portraits."

Thomas held out the key. "Since you're been conducting such thorough searches, why don't you look through the desks and I'll go to supper."

"Because I'm in charge of this mission, my friend," he said, clamping a hand on Thomas's shoulder. "And therefore, you're the one with the stomach ailment." Nicolas didn't mention that *he* was experiencing an annoying stomach ailment. It was driving him mad, but each time he thought of the proof he might uncover in the end, his entrails tightened.

"Ah. Yes. I see your point." Thomas's arm dropped to his side. Disappointment was evident in his eyes and Nicolas suspected it had something to do with Camille. "Do you want me to search Anne's desk, too?"

"No!" Nicolas mentally cringed at how strongly that came out.

Thomas lifted a brow.

Nicolas cleared his throat. "I'll take care of Anne's desk and her rooms. Search her sisters' rooms, desks, everything. Keep the key. I'll get it from you in the morning." If Thomas found evidence implicating one of the other two, he wouldn't have to search in Anne's private domain. "Make certain you leave nothing unturned."

CHAPTER SEVEN

Nicolas's heart rate doubled as he approached Anne's door.

Supper had been long and drawn out. Being forced to make witty commentary and polite conversation, with Anne so near, had been maddening.

Her cheeks slightly flushed, her breaths slightly quickened, she'd looked achingly beautiful. And—God help him—aroused by his presence at the table. He'd been impatient for the ordeal to be over, so that he could join her in her rooms. Each time her eyes met his, a bolt of heat shot through him. Starved for her, he'd barely touched his food. He couldn't get the image out of his mind of her on the desk in the library, her sweet body half exposed, her glistening pink sex slick with desire, looking every bit like every man's fantasy.

Because Anne and her sisters had been in their rooms all afternoon and he couldn't search Henriette's chambers as he'd wished to, he'd had to find other ways to fill the long hours before he'd be with Anne. Caring nothing about the books in the trunk—his grandmother's favorites—he was drawn to Anne's volume of poems.

He'd reread them.

And he shouldn't have.

Her words had affected him more strongly this time. This time he found them even more moving than before. Because this time he knew the woman behind the words. Her smile. Her voice. Her taste. Intimately.

Her heart was on those pages. But her heart had changed. She didn't believe in love anymore. It was absurd that the notion continued to bother him but he couldn't shake it. A heart that had had such depth had closed itself off. It was a shame.

Worse, rereading her work, knowing now that she'd had some intimate experience with men, had stirred up suspicions he'd spent most of the day trying to mute. He refused to believe Anne was Leduc without definitive proof.

Entertaining thoughts of his mission only aggravated that annoying emotion in his gut that wouldn't go away. He had absolutely nothing to feel guilty about. He was not the guilty party here—and yet he was left wrestling with that very emotion that directly clashed with his longing for her.

Nicolas reached Anne's door.

In short, he'd been in turmoil when he'd walked into the *Salle de Buffet* for supper, and he was in turmoil now.

He took a deep breath and let it out slowly.

On the other side of this door is an alluring woman no man would refuse to bed. She's waiting for you, warm and willing. Knock on the bloody door!

He rapped on the door lightly.

It flew open and he was yanked inside. The door slammed shut. Shoved hard, his back slammed against it. Nicolas grunted. It took a moment for his eyes to adjust to the dimmer light in the room.

Anne stood before him, hair down in long fiery-colored curls, wearing nothing but her chemise, her palms pressing against his chest.

He feasted on the sight of her. He had to remember to breathe. *Jésus-Christ*, she looked incredible.

She frowned. "What took you so long?"

He swallowed before he could summon his voice. "I—"

She shot to the balls of her feet, crushed her warm mouth against his, and thrust her tongue between his lips, and he forgot what he was going to say. Her taste was inebriating. He felt an instant hot rush through his veins.

She stroked his tongue with zealous swirls and mind-bending sucks, kissing him with magnificent intensity. He hauled her up against him, his cock pulsing between them, and trailed his hands down her back, returning her famished kiss with equal hunger. He couldn't seem to get enough. Not of this woman. Skimming his fingers up under her short chemise, he was stunned to find his hands on her pert—and very bare—derrière. *Dieu*, she wasn't wearing any *caleçons*.

She pulled away abruptly.

He reached out to drag her back, but she shook her head.

"Take this off." She was already pulling off his justacorps, her breaths as rapid and rough as his own.

Nicolas shrugged the knee-length jacket off his shoulders. Before the garment even hit the floor, her hands were tugging at the fastenings on his breeches, trying to open them.

He loved it when a woman got straight to the point.

Her fingers fumbled. He brushed them aside and opened his breeches in haste.

She pulled his shirttails out. He yanked his shirt off and discarded it.

Anne froze, her gaze slowly moving over his chest, down to his aching erection now straining out of his breeches. He was so hard, his cock felt as heavy as lead.

"You are more beautiful than any man has the right to be," she breathed.

Before he could respond to her endearing comment, her soft fingers wrapped around his erection and slowly pumped his prick. His words were lost in his groan. He closed his eyes and leaned heavily against the door, basking in the sensations radiating along his cock with each stroke of her hand.

Her other hand slipped inside his open breeches and cradled his sac, gently caressing him. "I want to pleasure you, Nicolas."

Oh, she was going to pleasure him, all right. Satiate him fully. He'd see to it. Then finally, *finally* this lust that had invaded his mind and was torturing his body would dissipate. He'd at last have it under control and be able to think clearly once more.

Suddenly, her hands were gone. His eyes flew open, dazed, his body rioting for more. He found her kneeling before him, the candlelight in the room giving her bright beautiful hair a bedazzling glow.

She grasped the base of his shaft and licked her lips.

Essence oozed from the tip of his eager cock as thoughts of feeding his length into her mouth burned in his mind.

Nicolas delved his fingers into her hair. This was not what he'd intended when he first walked in. Thanks to her parting words in the library, all he'd thought of the rest of the day was being inside her juicy core, riding her hard. But the famished look in her eyes and the lure of that hot wet mouth were . . . irresistible.

He brought his prick closer to her moist lips. "Are you hungry for my cock, Anne?"

Anne squeezed her knees together, trying to find relief from the throbbing ache between her legs. Yes, she was hungry for it! She was ravenous for him. Seeing how aroused she made him had her on fire and filled her with an exhilarating sense of power. She wanted him in her mouth. She wanted him filling her sex with that thick glorious part of his male anatomy.

Undaunted by his size and her limited experience, she said firmly, "Yes. Tonight, it's all mine to pleasure." She should have been shocked by her words, her brazen behavior, but wasn't. It thrilled her to see his eyes darken and feel his shaft twitch in her hand.

He brought out a side of her she never knew existed. She had no idea how he drew it out of her—so effortlessly, when no one else ever had—but she was grateful for the remarkable revelation.

"We're not stopping at tonight," he wickedly promised. "We're going to have at each other until we're both sated."

His words sent a hot shiver through her body. Briefly, she wondered how long it would take to satisfy the hunger she had for this man.

"Tell me if this pleases you." She swirled her tongue around the engorged tip of his shaft. He grunted sharply. Hiding her smile, she moistened her lips, then closed them over the crest of his sex. His breath hissed out through clenched teeth, his reaction causing her nipples to tighten and her core to cream. The sudden surge of desire made her light-headed.

"Take more," he growled.

His feral state was an aphrodisiac. She slid him farther into the wet heat of her mouth, drew him out, then plunged him back in deeper still, growing more and more emboldened and sure of her actions. His hips jerked.

He swore softly. His control snapped. Rearing back, he pushed back in, her mouth widening to accommodate him. He began to thrust. She matched his rhythm, her tongue caressing the underside of his penis with each rhythmic stroke as she sucked and sucked and sucked on him. The taste of his surrender was sweet. A moan, a sound of pure pleasure, escaped her throat and drew a hearty groan from him.

Anne slid her hands inside his breeches to grip his buttocks, his muscles tightening under her fingers. She held on to him, listening to his ragged breaths, keeping to the pace he desired.

He slowed his movements.

"Anne . . . I'm going to come . . . hard . . . in your mouth. If you don't want that, you've got to stop *now*." He stopped thrusting, his body straining with effort.

Her heart pounding, she responded by tightening her hold and drawing him in and out of her mouth, hard and fast, refusing to stop. He stiffened, his head falling back against the door. A guttural sound erupted out of him as spurt after spurt of come shot into her mouth and down her throat. She drank him in, digging her nails into him, wanting all he had, taking everything he gave, until his fingers loosened in her hair, his body relaxed, and she'd taken his last drop.

Slouched against the door, his breaths were short and shallow, his muscled chest rising and falling rapidly.

Drawing his sex from her mouth, Anne rose on shaky limbs, reeling, licking a small drop of his essence from her bottom lip. His eyes were closed, and on his handsome face was the undeniable expression of rapture.

She'd done that to him. Joy filled every empty chamber in her heart. Making him desperate for her had been, as he'd said, a "heady rush."

He opened his eyes, his usual knee-weakening half-smile forming on his lips the moment he met her gaze.

Nicolas pulled her to him. He was amazed at the transformation in her and delighted in it. No longer hiding behind a façade—the cool erudite author—she'd embraced the passion that was so much a part of her.

And dear God, there was such perfect passion between them.

She laced her arms around his neck, a grin on her face despite the carnal need he saw in her eyes.

"You liked that," she stated, looking adorably pleased with herself.

That was an understatement. He couldn't recall the last time he'd come that hard. At least now, the edge had been taken off his lust.

"Really? What makes you think so?" he teased, unable to keep the mirth from his tone.

She snuggled closer, her soft bottom giving a sweet little wiggle. "I suppose it's just a guess," she teased back.

He chuckled. She felt so good in his arms.

She caressed his cheek, her smile fading. "Thank you, Nicolas."

He furrowed his brow. "For what?"

"For showing me that there is more to physical intimacies between men and women than I ever knew. In fact, I never would have believed it had I not enjoyed it firsthand. What we've done today is a first for me. I'd heard of such acts, but never experienced them. I'm glad I shared them with you."

Her words were touching, and he cautioned himself against having any more tender emotions where she was concerned.

He should take advantage of her amenable mood and draw information out of her. But he didn't want to ask questions related to Leduc. Or her past lovers. Not now. He nuzzled her neck, enjoying the way her silky hair felt against his face. He didn't want to spoil this moment and found himself wishing that there wasn't anything more complicated between them than their desire for each other. "There is still more to experience," he murmured. "Show me where the bed is."

He felt her shiver of excitement before she stepped back and took his hand. The chemise hid little from his view. Her nipples were pebbled and her shapely thighs were bare, looking satiny smooth. His semihard cock thickened.

He couldn't wait to nestle between those soft thighs, feel them wrapped around him.

They entered her bedchamber of soft pinks and light greens. She climbed onto the bed and was sitting on her heels in the middle, waiting for him, looking so lush.

At the foot of the bed, Nicolas began discarding the remainder of his clothing. Her lovely eyes moved over him, stopping on his cock. He loved the way she looked at him, with such hot need. *How will she look at you when she learns what you've been up to?* He abruptly arrested the errant thought.

Her delicate brows rose slightly. "You're already . . . uh . . ." Her voice trailed off. She was unbalanced and endearingly flustered again, her nervous excitement, tangible. Accustomed to women with a more casual attitude toward carnal encounters, he found her refreshingly different.

She is different. You'll likely be arresting one of her sisters soon. How often have you done that to a woman you've bedded? Nicolas cursed the mental distractions. That was later. The future was in the future. This was now. And at this moment, all he wanted was to be with this one incredibly sensuous, bright, beautiful woman.

"I've been hard for you for two days. One orgasm isn't going to be enough—even an orgasm by such a talented mouth."

Nicolas tossed the last of his apparel onto the floor. "Come here," he ordered, sinking his knees one at a time on the bed.

Her nipples were driving him mad. They strained for him against the soft material of her chemise, and he was going to give them all the carnal attention those luscious peaks deserved.

She moved close. He slipped her chemise off. Her arms were just about to circle his neck when he caught her wrists and held her arms apart.

He let his eyes drink her in, taking in every appealing curve of her body and the pretty auburn curls covering her sex, already moist from her juices.

He met her gaze, and realized she was watching him closely for his reaction. He wanted her to have no doubts as to what he thought. "You're breathtaking."

She looked a little embarrassed but mostly pleased by his comment. "So are you."

Dieu, she was sweet—and disquieting. His thoughts were far too jumbled and soft for his liking, and he decided to blame them on his yet unsatisfied appetite for the ravishing poetess.

She pressed her warm mouth to his and kissed him. Nicolas released her wrists and pulled her tightly against him, squeezing his cock between them. He groaned.

Finally he was going to bed her and end his obsession to have her.

Suddenly, she pushed away, taking him by surprise. His eyes snapped open.

"I have something I need to tell you about myself." Her hand was against his chest, staving him off. He didn't like the earnest expression on her face. "I want to be honest with you."

His stomach dropped. *No!* Given the timing, that was the very last thing he wanted from her. Whatever she was about to say, he had a feeling he didn't want to hear it.

Nicolas clasped her wrist and gently removed her hand from his chest. Slipping his other hand onto the nape of her neck, he pulled her closer, bringing her mouth to his. "Later. Not now," he murmured against her lips. "No confessions during sex. Just mutual pleasure."

"I am not a virgin," she blurted out.

He jerked his head up. *Merde.*

"I'm not sure if you've guessed it or not, but I wanted to tell you just the same."

"Fine. Good. It doesn't matter." But the voice inside him screamed otherwise, more suspicions about Leduc rushing through his mind. He crushed his mouth to hers, desperate to drown them out with a fresh wave of lust.

She cupped his face between her soft hands and pulled away again, her breathing as quickened as his own. "There's been only one other man, and he never bestowed the pleasure you have. I wanted you to know the truth." Then, she was back to kissing him, trailing hot wet kisses along his neck.

Nicolas closed his eyes. And even though his prick was as stiff as wood and his body achingly aroused once more, his mind balked. *Fuck. Not now!* He wanted carnal gratification. He wanted her. Not thoughts about the man she'd been with and what that may mean. Not thoughts about what he'd have to do if she turned out to be Leduc. Or how she'd react if instead he had to bring one of her beloved sisters before the King.

And especially—*most especially*—not the guilt over his lies.

He wanted to lose himself in the sweet sensations of her mouth, her touch. He took her hand and brought it to his cock. Her fingers immediately curled around him and gave a little squeeze. The sound of bliss escaped his lips. But as hot pleasure rippled through him, his mind refused to quiet, growing more insistent. Getting louder. And louder.

The next thing he knew, he was staring at her surprised expression; his hands were on her shoulders—and to his astonishment—he was holding her at arm's length.

Jésus-Christ, he'd just pushed her away.

"I need a moment," he tossed out, climbed off the bed, marched into the antechamber, and closed the doors.

CHAPTER EIGHT

In the antechamber, fire crackled in the hearth, the sound mingling with Nicolas's ragged breaths. Choking on his frustration and rage, he wanted to smash his fist against the wall. *What the hell are you doing? What is the matter with you? She's so damned desirable. She is hungry for it. This is no time for a crisis of conscience!*

He couldn't believe he was with a gorgeous woman. Naked. Painfully hard. And was actually hesitating to bed her.

Something caught the corner of his eye. The fire from the hearth cast an orange light into the two rooms that stemmed from the one he was in. In one of those rooms, he could clearly see a small writing desk. Some books were on it. As was a crystal inkwell. The desk had several drawers.

"Nicolas?" Anne's voice grabbed his attention. She stood at the door, and to his disappointment, she'd placed her chemise back on. "Is everything all right?"

No. Never, not ever in his life had he become discomposed—and certainly never during an intimate encounter. He was highly disciplined. Trained in combat. Skilled in weapons. And when he wasn't working toward his next ambitious promotion, he was participating in his favorite pastime—recreational sex.

He liked women. Loved a good tumble.

He didn't think he could be unraveled—by her or anyone. It horrified him that she had.

Anne approached and, by her expectant expression, was awaiting his response.

"I . . . uh . . ." *Dieu*, he was actually *flustered*. He gnashed his teeth.

Something flickered in her eyes. "Say no more. I know what you're after."

He tensed. "You do?"

"Yes. It's rather obvious." The knowing look in her eyes made him uneasy.

"It is?" It couldn't be. How could she possibly know a thing about his mission?

"Of course. It's why you came in here." She stepped between him and the rectangular wooden table in the middle of the room. "I know what you're looking for."

His eyes narrowed. "And what is it I'm looking for?" He'd be damned if he confessed a thing.

She lifted her brows. "You want me to say it?"

He curled his fingers under her chin. "Say it."

"The door you're looking for is over my shoulder—the *Salle de Bain*. You'll find the chamber pot in there, next to the tub."

Nicolas froze and blinked. Then he tossed his head back and roared with laughter at the sheer ridiculousness of the situation. "You think I need to . . . to . . ." He shook his head, unable to finish the sentence, laughter erupting from him again.

Perplexed, she frowned.

It took several moments before he could finally sober up. This was definitely not his typical sexual encounter. It was high time to put an end to his imbecilic behavior.

He picked her up and placed her bottom down on the table behind her. Her eyes widened. Nicolas cradled her face between his palms. "I came in here because you overwhelm me."

Her eyes softened. "You overwhelm me, too." She smiled. "And I rather like it. I want to be overwhelmed some more."

He liked her answer. Actually, there was a lot about her he liked.

"Good. Because I'm going to take you—*slowly*." Nicolas pulled off her chemise and dropped it onto the table. "Would you like that, Anne? Would you like to be fucked slowly?"

Her breathing had begun to escalate.

"Yes."

Nicolas reached behind her and slid her derrière closer to the edge of the table. "Show me how wet you are for me. Spread your thighs nice and wide." He took a step back.

She paused, and he got the sense she was wrestling with inhibition.

"Do it," he prompted softly.

Slowly, she parted her thighs.

"That's good, Anne. Lean back."

His heart raced as he watched her place her palms down on the table behind her, her hips now perfectly angled for his viewing pleasure.

Her sex glistened with her juices. Unable to resist, he scored his finger from her moist opening up to her clit, stopping to press on the sensitive nub with enough pressure to make her gasp in delight.

"I'm going to take you right now." His cock jerked.

"Nicolas . . ." Her thighs trembled. "There's a bed . . ."

"Next time." He hadn't intended to have her on a hard surface again, but he'd finally quieted his brain. He wasn't going to do anything to disturb the delicious desire flowing between them or jeopardize this incredible experience with this intoxicating female. "It will be just as good. I promise."

He'd make her forget any discomfort she felt.

Taking his prick in hand, he guided it to her slick entrance. Her head fell back with a soft moan. A tremor of expectation quivered through her and radiated up his cock. He shuddered. Oh, how she turned him inside out. It felt as though he'd waited forever for this. For her. He had to have her. Or die.

Gripping her hips, he pressed into her, watching as the crest of his cock sank into her wet heat. He was thick and full and she was so deliciously snug. Pleasure roared through his system. His heart hammered hard. He pushed, sinking deeper, her juices coating his cock. Taking his time, he stretched her slowly, savoring the stunning sensations along his prick as she enveloped him an inch at a time. She whimpered and lowered herself onto her back, trembling.

A bead of sweat formed on his forehead. He continued his steady progress, bearing down on her, unrelenting. "You're going to take all of me, aren't you, Anne? You want it all, don't you?"

She panted, lolling her head to one side. *"Yes . . ."*

Nicolas butted against the entrance of her womb and groaned. At his possession, she made the most sensual sound. He loved that. He loved everything about sex, not just the climax but all things preceding it. Especially the initial penetration, that first thrust—fast or slow—that buried him inside. And being inside Anne, feeling the hot clasp of her tight sex clenched around him, the light quivering of her inner muscles along his length, was more heaven than any man deserved.

She was primed. He knew it wouldn't take much to send her over the edge.

Leaning forward, he grasped the edge of the table with one hand and slipped his other arm under her waist, arching her body to him. He latched onto her breast and suckled hard. She cried out, her fingers tangling in his hair, her sensitive teat instantly distending in his mouth.

Sucking and lightly biting her nipple, he pumped his cock in her, giving her short shallow thrusts that kept her enthralled, but also kept her from coming. She mewed in protest and strained toward him, trying to draw in him deeper. Her efforts were futile. He wouldn't acquiesce. He continued, his measured strokes unbroken. Not wanting this to end.

"Nicolas . . . please . . ." She wrapped her legs around him, still desperately squirming and arching.

Releasing her nipple from the confines of his mouth, he flicked it with his tongue. "Please what? Please, make me come,

Nicolas? Please, fuck me harder?" Turning to her other nipple, he lightly raked his teeth across it.

She gasped. "Yes, to all that. *Right. Now!*"

Nicolas lifted his head, softly chuckling. "So fiery. And impassioned. I like that . . ." He gave her a deep thrust before returning to his shorter strokes.

She made a frustrated sound. "Nicolas, if you make me wait any longer, I swear, I'll—I'll . . . make you pay."

"Mmmm, now that sounds delicious." He suckled her breast gently with just the right amount of finesse to snatch her breath away. "How will you make me pay?" He drew her hardened nipple back into his mouth.

"I'm a writer . . . I have . . . *ahhhh* vivid imagination . . . I'll . . . think of something."

With his cock dipped in glory, and this passionate woman pleading for more, Nicolas ceded. He slipped his arm out from under her, straightened, and grasped her hips again. Suddenly, he didn't want to make her wait. He wanted to give her all the pleasure she craved and more. To make this an unforgettable experience for her.

Tilting her hips, he plunged, driving the full length of his cock inside her. Her sharp cry of pleasure resonated in the room.

Briefly, he closed his eyes, unable to move or breathe as his own wave of hot pleasure crested over him.

Tightening his grasp, he plunged again, and began giving her deep solid thrusts. "How does that feel?" By the sultry sounds she made, by the way she flexed her legs and squeezed them around him, he knew she liked the depth and angle of his thrusts, but he wanted to hear her say it. "Tell me, *chère.*"

A light sheen of perspiration glistened on her flushed skin. Her eyes were closed, her sweet breasts jiggling with the force of each downstroke.

"So. Good," she said, each word rushing out on a pant.

She clenched around his thrusting prick, tearing a growl from his throat. He reveled in the decadent sensations washing through him. He could never tire of this. Never tire of her.

She was his. His sensual soul mate.

His perfect match.

Nicolas released her hips. "Come here," he said hoarsely, and grasping her wrists, he pulled her up, dragged her closer, and drove his cock into her with such intensity it made them both gasp. Fisting her hair with his one hand, the other splayed against her lower back, he rode her with fast powerful plunges, holding nothing back. He thrust his tongue into her mouth, wanting to possess every part of her. To his delight, she returned his voracious kiss, feeding his frenzy.

He felt her arms slide around him, her heels dig into his backside. She held on, her lush form enveloping him completely. Breaking the kiss, she moved her hot hungry mouth along his jaw, toward his ear.

The pressure in his sac was exquisite torture, his body raging for release.

"Nicolas, I think I'm going to . . . I'm truly . . . actually going to . . . to . . ."

Christ, she was on the edge. So was he. "Do it. Let yourself go." Her sweet, perfect cunt was quivering around him. Still ramming her, he pushed up against her clit, and then again, adding jolting sensations without breaking his rhythm. "Come!"

She lurched sharply in his arms. Throwing her hips forward and her head back, she screamed, her orgasm wracking her body. Nicolas tightened his hold and clenched his teeth, glorious spasms suddenly assailing his plunging cock, her sweet sheath sucking at his shaft, pulling and pulsing around him in mind-melting waves. Each knee-weakening contraction squeezed him so fiercely it made his prick throb. He battled back his release, refusing to let go, determined to enjoy her orgasm—the engulfing sensations coursing along his cock—before he indulged in his own.

He pumped his hips as the spasms faded, but then she jerked and gave him an unexpected firm clench that hurled him over the edge. Hot come rushed down his cock.

He reared just in time. Semen shot from him with stunning force. Burying his face in her soft hair, he shuddered and groaned, come purging from his prick in draining spurts, euphoria flooding his body.

Dieu, he didn't want this to end, and he knew he was referring to more than just the sex act.

Finally spent, his legs shaking, his breathing as erratic as hers, Nicolas lifted his head and met her gaze.

A smile shone on her beautiful face.

"I've never felt anything like that," she whispered.

Neither had he. Softly, he kissed her mouth, sounds of contentment emanating from them both. This was unlike any sexual experience he'd ever had. It was more than just a sating of his body. The fulfillment he felt went as deep as his heart and soul.

He needed more of this. More of her.

He'd found the perfect bliss.

*****

"What do you mean, *nothing?*" Nicolas asked Thomas, incredulous.

"I mean, *nothing.*"

"You checked every drawer in Henriette's desk?"

"Yes."

"And all over her rooms?"

"Yes! I checked everywhere," Thomas snapped, looking uncharacteristically haggard this morning. "There was *nothing.*" He slammed the key down on the table in Nicolas's rooms and marched away.

Nicolas had hoped all the evidence he needed would be in Henriette's private quarters. Damn it, where was she hiding her notes, her drafts?

What if it's not Henriette at all? His stomach clenched. It would be difficult enough to arrest one of Anne's sisters. But to have to arrest Anne. Beautiful Anne. His Anne. Images of last night, of her, of her in his arms, filled his mind and made him ache.

He glanced up at Thomas and caught him raking a hand through his hair as he paced near the windows.

"What is it, Thomas?"

Stopping in his tracks, Thomas exhaled sharply and turned to look out the window.

Nicolas approached. Something was amiss. "Thomas?" He placed a hand on his friend's shoulder. His body stiff, his jaw tight, Thomas met his gaze.

"You found something in Camille's rooms, didn't you?" Nicolas asked.

Thomas returned his attention to the window, staring blankly at the courtyard below. For a moment, Nicolas thought he wasn't going to respond, but then, ever so slightly, he nodded. "I haven't been able to sleep all night."

Nicolas's heart raced. "What did you find?"

Keeping his eyes straight ahead, Thomas responded, "Camille came to my rooms after supper. I'd just finished invading her privacy, reading the contents of her desk, looking for possible evidence to arrest her, and she was worried about me. Concerned for my welfare. Do you know what that made me feel like?"

Nicolas had a very strong idea.

Thomas turned to him, his expression rueful. "I kissed her, Nicolas. I shouldn't have, but I couldn't help myself. I'm not like you, my friend. You can kiss a woman, even bed her, and remain detached. You don't let anything distract you or get in the way of doing His Majesty's bidding. I can't do that. I can't act. Nor be indifferent. I'm a failure as a Musketeer."

Nicolas was failing, too. Failing to accomplish his objectives. And worst of all, failing to keep the soft sentiment Anne inspired at bay. He'd made love to her multiple times last night. The more he'd had her last eve, the more he wanted her.

Everything she did, everything she said, stirred tender feelings he couldn't quell.

He had not remained detached.

Nor had he used last night's situation to his advantage as he'd intended—to gain information. He'd never questioned her once the entire night. Hadn't wanted to.

Couldn't bring himself to.

"Nicolas, I found Camille's old journal." Thomas's voice was quiet. "Many of the entries were filled with venom directed toward her late brother-in-law, the Baron de Pierpont, for his treatment of Henriette, and toward a gentleman named Roland d'Orsay."

"Who is Roland d'Orsay?"

"The third son of the Comte de Galard. Apparently, he charmed Anne, made promises he never intended to keep, claimed her maidenhead, and then married another."

Nicolas chest tightened.

Roland d'Orsay. The man she'd mentioned last night.

Not only had d'Orsay denied her carnal pleasure in bed, but he'd deceived her. Used her. *Jésus-Christ*, no wonder she had such a lowly opinion of men.

And yet, she set aside her biases to be with you.

Nicolas felt like a scoundrel of the highest order. And though he reminded himself that he was on a mission for his King—it did nothing to combat the self-condemnation welling inside him.

He was using her. And it bothered him when it shouldn't. When it couldn't.

When there was the chance she was the one he might have to arrest.

"I didn't think sweet Camille had it in her to loathe so deeply. I have a terrible feeling that Leduc is Camille." Thomas shook his head. "This is not just a mission anymore. I'm fond of her. I like all three of them. *Seigneur Dieu*, I even like Henriette. How can we do this? How can we arrest any of them? How can I arrest Camille?" Thomas hung his head.

"We have a duty to uphold." He'd forced each word off his tongue. He was fond of Camille, too. Nicolas had no idea how he'd arrest Camille either. But he knew he could manage it. In fact, he knew he could manage to do just about anything, except arrest Anne.

"We need something more conclusive than some old journal entries," Nicolas was constrained to add. "It isn't enough proof."

"I didn't find anything else. What about Anne? Have you searched her rooms and desk?"

His body turned rigid. "No. You had the key, remember?"

Thomas walked over to the table, picked up the key, and returning with it, placed it on his palm. "Well, you have it back. Now there is nothing to stop you from examining the contents of her desk."

Nicolas looked at the small gold key.

Burdened with what he had to do, it felt heavy in his hand.

It burned his palm.

CHAPTER NINE

"I've been cast aside!" Madame de Boutette sniffled, wiping her tears with a lace handkerchief. "I've been completely and utterly replaced by that whore, Pauline Pradeau. She's bewitched him, I tell you."

Anne fought back a second yawn. For the last few glorious nights, Nicolas had given her little rest—and more bliss than any heart could hold.

"I have been with him for years," Madame de Boutette continued, her tone getting increasingly angrier. "I was his favorite mistress. Now he favors another. After I've endured all of his disgusting habits, and amorous encounters of the blandest sort! Do you have any idea how dull and distasteful it is to bed the Marquis de Ranvier?"

"No, madame. I don't." Anne dipped her quill in the inkwell and wrote, "*Ranvier has disgusting habits. Is dull and distasteful to bed.*"

"Well, then allow me to tell you that I've had to moan and carry on as if . . ."

Madame's words drifted away as images of Nicolas and memories of her moaning and carryings-on in his arms ran through her mind and quickened her pulse. Every reaction he drew from her was real and sublime. She loved how insatiable he was around her. How wonderful it felt to be so desired.

How wonderful it was just to be with him.

During their short time together she'd transformed. For the better. Her heart and soul felt light, and she had Nicolas to thank. What was just as incredible, she'd begun to do something she'd completely abandoned and had lost all desire for after Roland; she'd started writing poetry again.

She'd forgotten how much pleasure it brought her. Wanting his reaction, last eve she'd worked up the courage to show Nicolas her new poems. Poems she hadn't even told her sisters about.

By his expression, his eyes, and his words, he adored them; his praise of her work filled her with as much joy as his kisses and touch. Everything was so perfect between them, except . . . something was bothering him. If only she knew what.

He denied it. Hid it. In fact, he hid it quite well. Yet she was attuned to it. She sensed it. Saw fleeting flashes of it in his eyes. And she didn't believe it had to do with his grandmother.

"He rarely bathes. It's like bedding a barnyard animal. And his rounded belly keeps getting in the way," Madame finished with a huff.

Anne sighed and put down her quill. "Madame, may I be frank?"

The woman who was only a few years older than Anne raised her brows. "Well . . . I suppose . . ."

"If the Marquis de Ranvier is so unappealing, why bemoan the end of the affair?"

"Well, because I love him! And he loves another. He's tossed me aside like a pair of old shoes."

"Love? You've described your *love* as a barnyard animal."

"That's because he smells like one."

"And his touch is unpleasant to you, correct?"

"Well, yes." Madame de Boutette smoothed her skirts. "It is."

"Madame, with all due respect, it's rather clear that it is your pride that's wounded, not your heart."

The woman's mouth fell agape.

Undaunted, Anne continued, "If you loved Ranvier, you wouldn't be repelled. In fact, you'd find him highly appealing.

You'd crave to be with him. As much as possible. The thought of him would make you happy, not sick. You'd want his touch. Enjoy his company, and cherish it."

Anne knew her speech was about more than the Marquis de Ranvier. It was about her feelings for Nicolas. She was in love with him. How could she not be?

Why shouldn't she allow herself to be?

She'd denied herself happiness long enough. Why shouldn't she take another chance on love? Love was worth the risk. As was Nicolas.

After what she'd been through with Roland, after witnessing Henriette's suffering, after hearing countless stories of other women's heartbreaks, Anne had become convinced that there wasn't an honorable man left in the realm.

But she'd had a change of heart. And she had Nicolas to thank for that as well.

With love inside her heart, there was no more room for the bitterness she'd harbored there. For the first time, the thought of writing a Gilbert Leduc tale—the particular kind of tale Madame de Boutette wanted her to write—left a sour taste in her mouth.

Anne rose. "Madame, go home, and find yourself someone worthy of your love. Do not despair over the loss of a man who causes you such distress. Consider yourself fortunate to be rid of him." It was the attitude she should have taken long ago with Roland. She'd been a colossal fool to allow Roland to make her miserable long after his departure. It was clear to her now that by clinging to her heartbreak, she'd actually held on to Roland, making him a part of her life when he didn't deserve to be.

Madame de Boutette stood up, looking aghast. "But—But what about my story? Monsieur Leduc?"

"Monsieur Leduc is quite fatigued." Anne ushered the woman to the main door of her apartments, knowing Vincent would show her out of the Comtesse's home.

"He is?"

"He's long overdue for a respite."

"Really?"

"Yes, and I can't say when or if he'll be ready to write again." At least not stories for embittered hearts. She wouldn't do it. She'd talk to her sisters and the Comtesse. Leduc was going to be much more selective. If Leduc's stories were to continue, they'd have to be fewer and only in instances where a woman found herself in truly dire circumstances—like poor Eléonore, Duchesse de Falloux, who was still unjustly confined to a convent.

The moment Madame de Boutette left, Anne moved toward her desk. She wanted to seek out Nicolas, perhaps spend the day with him, but couldn't. Leduc's book was due at the printer's soon and she needed to finish Eléonore's story.

Sitting down at her desk, Anne pulled out the draft of her work in progress and dipped her quill in the inkwell. When the Comtesse returned, Anne intended to talk to her about her grandson, and then tell Nicolas everything about Leduc.

She wanted no secrets between them.

She felt a smile tug at her lips. Nicolas would likely praise her for her stories as he had her poetry. He'd be completely understanding and utterly supportive of her efforts.

*****

Nicolas was smiling as his eyes tracked Anne in the crowded Salon. Another of his grandmother's Saturday Salons was under way. This one was just as crowded as the last.

He knew he should be mingling with his grandmother's friends. He was, after all, supposed to be interested in learning about the Comtesse and getting to know the people in her life. But he had no desire to make polite conversation. He was content to simply watch Anne as she moved from guest to guest, charming them all.

As with last week, Nicolas noted how the men looked at her. Their interest keen. Many made no attempt to hide their desire. But as they watched her, gaped at her, her attention, when she was not engaged in conversation, was directed at *him*.

Repeatedly, she'd turn, seek him out in the crowd, and smile when she met his gaze.

It sent a jolt of joy to his heart each time.

"Nicolas." He heard Thomas's voice.

Nicolas pulled his attention from Anne and found his friend standing beside him. "Where have you been?" he asked. Thomas had been missing all day. He'd learned from Vincent that he'd left the hôtel.

"I need to speak to you. Privately," Thomas said.

Nicolas didn't like the look on Thomas's face.

He led Thomas out of the Grand Salon, across the vestibule, and into the servants' stairwell. It was dark and quiet once he'd closed the door.

"What is it?" Nicolas hated the uneasy feeling building inside him.

Thomas rubbed the back of his neck. "I couldn't take it anymore, Nicolas. All this deceit with Camille is getting to me. I left to clear my head. Before I knew it, I found myself at the Arsenal. Tiersonnier was there. He demanded to know about the mission."

Nicolas tensed. "What did you tell him?"

"That you had things well in hand, but . . . that didn't satisfy him. He pressed for more information. He wants this matter done."

"Go on," Nicolas prompted, seeing there was more that Thomas wasn't saying.

Thomas looked away. That wasn't a good sign. Nicolas's stomach tightened.

"He demanded details," Thomas said, not meeting his gaze.

"*And?*"

"And I told him . . .where you were. Who—Who we suspected was Leduc."

Nicolas grabbed his lapels and shoved him against the wall. "You did *what?*"

Thomas's eyes widened. "We have sworn an oath. Did you want me to lie to the commander of the Guard?"

Yes! Nicolas took a long deep breath and let it out slowly. By force of will, he uncurled his hands and released his friend. "No."

"You've had the key for days, Nicolas. Have you searched Anne's desk yet?"

"I have not had the key for days," he responded sharply. "I told you the other day that she noticed the key was missing. I had to toss it onto the floor in the library, so she'd think she lost it there. The library was the last place she'd seen it."

"That was two days ago. The key is back in her locket. You're fucking her, for God's sake."

"And your point is?"

"Surely during the time you've spent in her rooms, you've had an opportunity or two to take the key and have a glance at the desk?"

Nicolas's eyes narrowed. "I have not had the opportunity." *Liar.* He was avoiding the desk. Avoiding the search.

"This mission cannot continue indefinitely."

"I will get to the desk, when I can. Until then—"

"You have one more day," Thomas blurted out.

"What do you mean, *one more day?*"

"Tiersonnier said if you don't make your arrest by then, he'll send Musketeers here to search for the evidence and to bring in Leduc."

The look of horror must have been on his face. Thomas's gaze shot down to his feet. "I'm sorry." His voice was a whisper. Or maybe it simply sounded faint with the blood roaring in Nicolas's ears.

Thomas reached into his justacorps and pulled out a gold key. "I managed to get this from Camille." He handed the key to Nicolas. "Anne, Camille, and Henriette are busy with the guests. I'll make sure no one goes upstairs. This is an ideal time to search Anne's rooms and desk."

Nicolas's heart plummeted. He knew Thomas was right.

He couldn't avoid the task any longer.

He had to learn once and for all what was in Anne's desk.

*****

Nicolas leaned against the doorway in Anne's antechamber looking at the desk he had to search.

Anne's rooms were quiet and still. The air, without her there, was thick and hard to breathe. This was the last thing he wanted to do, his every instinct screaming, *"Don't look!"*

Nicolas glanced back at the bed in the bedchamber. For the first time in his life, he wasn't simply having sex with a woman. There was emotion involved. He was making love. And he'd found the intimate encounters and the time he spent with her far more pleasurable and gratifying than he could have ever imagined.

He didn't want what he had with Anne to be over. But he knew, as he stood holding the key in his fist, that their time together was running out.

There wasn't a thing he could do about it.

It sickened him to know that soon her warm looks, her soft words, her kisses, would vanish. In their place, he'd have her disdain. It didn't matter who Leduc was. No matter whom he arrested, she'd feel betrayed. Deceived. Despise him for his numerous lies.

Thomas was right. Nicolas hadn't been doing his duty. He'd procrastinated simply to delay the inevitable.

He'd done the unimaginable; he'd allowed feelings to be fostered for a beautiful red-haired poetess who was like no woman he'd ever known.

And a suspect.

He was under the King's command. If he didn't do this, it would be done just the same.

Pushing himself toward the desk, Nicolas approached it with dread. Slowly, he sat down, took a deep breath before he inserted the key, and unlocked the first drawer.

Jésus-Christ, the best he could hope for in this dismal situation was that the author wasn't Anne.

Sliding open the drawer, he then pulled out the contents: a small stack of parchments. Upon close scrutiny, he realized they were poems. New poetry. Despite the trepidation he felt, a small smile pulled at the corners of his mouth. She'd been so joyful about her new poems. He'd been moved and honored that she'd wanted to show them to him.

She had a gift for writing poetry, and they were as lovely as she was.

He checked the next drawer, and the next, growing ever more hopeful with each one that yielded no evidence of Leduc.

Turning the key in the final lock of the final drawer, Nicolas opened it and found parchments and a ledger. He pulled them out. The words "Eléonore, Duchesse de Falloux" were across the top of the first parchment.

He scrutinized the writings on the loose parchments, and then the contents of the ledger, his heart sinking lower and lower. Each page that condemned her consumed him with grief and tore him apart.

He closed the ledger.

Closed the drawer.

Closed his eyes, and hung his head.

*****

Anne grinned the moment she spotted Nicolas in her rooms. "There you are!"

Seated near the hearth in her antechamber staring at the fire, he looked up at her and smiled. But his smile didn't reach his eyes.

His light gray eyes were rueful.

Her grin had completely dissolved by the time she reached him. "Nicolas, is everything all right?"

He pulled her onto his lap and drew her close, his sad smile still on his lips. "It is tonight." Lightly, he ran his knuckles along her cheek.

She wasn't sure what he meant. She wrapped her arms around his broad shoulders. "Something is bothering you and has been for some time. Tell me what it is. Perhaps I can help."

He shook his head. "In the morning . . . We'll talk in the morning. This night belongs to us. I want nothing to interfere with it. Or spoil it."

What could spoil it? she wanted to ask, but he threaded his fingers through her hair and pulled her forward. Their mouths met and her thoughts scattered. An intoxicating rush of arousal and emotion flooded her body. Her nerve endings sparked to life. Parting her lips for him, she welcomed his tongue into her mouth, stroking it, caressing it, loving his taste, his scent, the sounds of his escalating breaths. She loved his every heated reaction to her.

She loved him.

"Tonight you are all mine," he murmured and kissed her harder, with enough intensity to make her head spin.

Vaguely, she felt him lift her in his arms. He deposited her onto the bed with infinite care, then straightened. His hands moved to the fastenings on his breeches. Sitting up, she watched him undress, transfixed. Expectant.

Nicolas yanked off his shirt. His sculpted chest, his strong body were mesmerizing to behold, and protruding from his open breeches was his sizable sex, the sight of which made her both hungry and weak.

As soon as he was naked, she rose to her knees, her heart giving a small flutter of joy. He knelt on the bed in front of her, cradled her face between his palms, and gave her a long languid kiss. It was only when he pulled away that she realized he'd released her cheeks and had opened her bodice. Anne quickly helped as he pulled and tugged, tossing off article after article until she, too, was naked.

He moved his gaze over her, slowly, in a way he never had before. He took his time to take her in, as if he was trying to commit her to memory.

"How will I ever stop wanting you?" he whispered, seemingly more to himself than to her.

"You don't have to stop." She smiled. "In fact, I'd prefer it if you didn't."

"Ah, Anne, I'd love that." He caressed the outside curve of her breast, then cupping her, grazed his thumb over her hardened nipple. She jolted at the lush sensation. "I'd love this to go on forever." His thumb continued its delicious torment. Her sex moistened and contracted.

"I have no objections to something more indefinite."

"I pray you'll always feel that way." He threaded the fingers of his free hand in her hair. "I never expected to find a woman like you here."

He lowered her onto her back and covered her with his hard body, the delectable press of his muscled form sending hot tingles through her.

Resting on his elbows, he said in all earnest, "This passion, desire, the . . . emotions between us . . . are all real. I don't want you ever to doubt that, no matter what happens. I want you to remember how good it is between us. Promise me you'll always remember how you feel right now. How incredible it feels when we're together." He brushed his lips over hers. "Promise me, Anne."

"Nicolas, what are you trying to say?" She couldn't quell the unease that was beginning to permeate her.

"I want you to promise you'll remember this night—all the nights we've shared—and how perfect they were. Promise me."

She stared up into his beseeching eyes, unsure of what to make of him tonight.

He dipped his head and kissed the sensitive spot beneath her ear. "*Promise*, Anne." Lightly, he bit her earlobe, his knees spreading her thighs wide apart. She shivered.

"I promise. I won't forget."

"Not ever." He stroked his thick solid shaft along her folds, her body bathing him with her juices.

"Never."

"I need to have you." He dipped his head lower still and gave her shoulder a tiny bite. She moaned and surged against him, the sensation of his cock gliding over her sensitive nub and needy flesh sending frissons of pleasure streaking straight into her core.

"I need you right now," he said.

He'd planted the head of his shaft firmly against her opening and pushed inside. Thank God, he didn't make her wait. Her body opened and gave way to his possession. The steady pressure as he slowly filled her was glorious.

With a flex of his hips, he butted hard against her womb. She gasped. He had her deliciously pinned to the bed. Her sex squeezed around him.

"*Jésus-Christ*, you feel so good," he groaned, giving her slow solid thrusts, increasing her fever. "So warm . . . silky . . . tight. *Dieu*, so tight. Let me feel it, Anne. Let me feel those delicious little clenches around my cock. Bear down on me, *chère*."

She tightened and released her inner muscles, reveling in the way he growled and groaned, lost to his desire for her, his cock driving into her faster and faster.

He swore. "I'm having you again"—he thrust—"and again. All night."

"Yes . . ." she panted out.

She loved him with her body, her hands, her mouth, kissing, tasting, lost to the friction, the frenzy of their lovemaking. She relished the feelings he'd awakened in her, feelings that swirled around her heart. She relished him, without words, just actions, caressing him, milking him. Knowing she was barreling toward a powerful release.

He captured her nipple between his finger and thumb and lightly pulled then pinched. A shock of pleasure shot through her. She came with a scream, uncontrollable shudders rolling though her body.

He roared her name, his thrusts unrelenting. Just as the spasms inside her faded, he jerked his length out and crushed her to him. Grinding his cock between their bodies, he let out a primitive growl, hot semen pouring onto her stomach as a tremor and then another jolted him. She held him tightly until at last he relaxed, their breathing slowly returning to normal. Caressing his back, she felt sated and languorous, basking in a wonderful sense of peace in the quiet afterglow.

He lifted his head. His tender smile moved her to one as well.

"Do you have any idea what you do to me?" he asked.

"I think I have some idea."

He chuckled. She loved the sound of his soft laugh.

Nicolas snagged his discarded shirt, rolled onto his back, and wiping them both clean, tossed it to the floor.

Lying on his back, he rolled her on top of him, her breasts pressing on his chest. He tucked a lock of her hair behind her ear. "You are extraordinary. More than any man could ever be fortunate enough to have and hold," was the last thing he said before he kissed her.

Anne lost track of time, unsure how long they lay naked, simply kissing, each one stirring her heart and reawakening her desire.

I love you . . . The words were on the tip of her tongue. Words she never thought she'd utter to any man ever again.

Tomorrow. She'd tell him tomorrow. He wanted to talk. And she decided she, too, had something to say.

Chapter Ten

Nicolas woke up in an empty bed. A sharp stab of disappointment cut into his heart. He wanted to wake up with Anne by his side. He wanted to squeeze out a final few tender moments before everything imploded on him. But Anne was probably with her sisters, writing.

Writing under the name "Gilbert Leduc."

Closing his eyes, he felt grief-stricken and cold. But not cold enough to numb or in any way lessen the suffocating misery inside him.

There was no getting out of what he had to do today.

What could he say to her? How on earth was he going to do this? He had no idea what the King would do with Anne once he brought her in.

A week ago, being in the King's private Guard was everything to him. He never thought there would ever come a day when he hated being a Musketeer. But he hated it now. He loathed it. With all of his being and every piece of his breaking heart.

Nicolas forced himself out of bed. His thoughts awhirl and his agony steadily rising, he went through the motions of washing and dressing. By the time he'd left Anne's rooms and reached the bottom of the grand stairwell, the pain inside him was excruciating. He'd rather face his own arrest than arrest her.

If only it were an option.

Looking for Thomas—praying he'd say something to Nicolas that would make this easier—he crossed the vestibule and froze when he heard Anne's voice.

"I don't believe it!" he heard her say. She was in the library.

A woman responded, "I'm afraid it's true." Her voice was unfamiliar.

Unable to turn back, constrained to push forward, Nicolas moved his leaden legs and approached the room he'd find his Anne in.

Stopping just inside the threshold, he was met with a jarring sight. Anne stood with her back to the windows, her eyes glistening with tears.

The moment her gaze met his, he lost his breath. *She knew.* It was etched on her expression and in the silent condemnation in her eyes.

He had no idea how she knew. But she did. *Dieu*, she did.

His eyes darted to his left. Henriette was seated on the settee with her arm around Camille. While Camille quietly wept, Henriette glowered at him with open contempt.

"Well, who do we have here?" A woman's voice snared his attention.

Nicolas's gaze shot to the right. There in the corner of the room stood a thin older woman. A lady, as her clothing indicated. His instincts told him this was the Comtesse de Cottineau.

His grandmother.

Anne approached him slowly, her breaths quick and shallow, her expression incredulous.

She stopped before him and stared at him as though he were a complete stranger, as if she were seeing him for the first time. As if he'd never been her lover. Had never held her in his arms. Had never loved her through the night. Many nights.

"You're . . ." She paused and took a deep breath before she began again. "Are you a *Musketeer?*" That last word was laced with a mixture of distress and disbelief.

He wanted to lie. He wanted to take her in his arms and hold her until the pain inside him subsided. But he couldn't do either.

He swallowed. "Yes."

Her beautiful mouth fell slightly agape. "Why—Why didn't you tell me?"

Nicolas clasped his hands before him to keep from reaching out and pulling her to him. He knew it was the very last thing she wanted at the moment. "Because I was—*am*—on a mission for His Majesty."

"*A mission?*" Her voice escalated. "What sort of mission are you on?" Her tone and demeanor told him she knew the answer—or at least suspected it. He glanced at the Comtesse.

Her expression hardened, and she had a knowing look in her gray eyes. He realized she'd been the one to tell Anne these details about him, but how did she know?

"Answer her," the Comtesse demanded. Nicolas would have done nothing, *absolutely nothing* the old woman asked of him, for he owed her nothing more than his disdain, but the request was for Anne. And for Anne, he'd do anything.

"I'm to determine who Gilbert Leduc is and bring him before the King," he said softly.

"So your coming here had nothing to do with getting to know your grandmother," Anne stated. It wasn't a question.

"No." He answered just the same. He owed her the whole truth.

"And you spent the entire time lying and scheming," Anne accused. He could tell she was fighting back her tears, trying to maintain the semblance of composure. He knew this was going to be bad, but in the thick of it, it was far worse than he'd imagined.

Nicolas lowered his eyes, because it was too painful to see her pain. "I have a duty to the King." He found himself despising those words more and more each time he uttered them.

"A duty?" She laughed, without mirth. "I see. And was it part of your duty to bed me?"

His gaze shot up to hers. Her eyes were narrow and she trembled with outrage.

"Anne, perhaps we can have this conversation in private."

"Why? My sisters and the Comtesse know what a fool I've been. What is there to hide? I must congratulate you. Your skill at duplicity is excellent. I actually believed you were different from other men. In truth, you are by far the most contemptible of the lot."

The lump welling in his throat rendered him momentarily speechless.

"You did not answer my question," Anne pressed sharply. "Was it part of your duty to bed me? Did the King request it of you?"

Dieu. "I am expected to do whatever it takes to accomplish my mission His Majesty."

"Well then, how wonderful for you. You got to indulge in some carnal diversions while you worked on your 'mission.'"

He hated the disgust in her tone, especially since she was speaking of their lovemaking. "What began as casual copulation became something . . . special."

"Oh, please," she scoffed. "Spare me more lies. What we did meant nothing to a man like you."

"That's not true. It meant—*means* a great deal to me. You mean a great deal to me."

She gave another hollow laugh. "Oh, of course. I mean so much to you that you have been conspiring and plotting against me, my sisters, and my patroness, stooping to trickery at every turn. Pray tell, when were you going to tell me the truth?"

"Today."

"And why today? What makes today so special?"

He didn't want to say it, but he didn't have a choice. He forced the words from his mouth. "I have to . . . make an arrest today."

Camille let out an audible sob and buried her face in Henriette's shoulder.

Anne didn't flinch. Stock-still, she said, "Well, it looks as though you are going to disappoint the King. Gilbert Leduc is not here. You're mistaken."

"That's right," Henriette concurred. "You are sadly mistaken."

"He is here," Nicolas gently countered Henriette. "He's in this room." He dragged his gaze back to Anne. "You are Leduc."

To her credit, she didn't crack or crumble before him. "You have no proof."

This was only becoming more and more torturous. "The proof is in your room, Anne. In your desk drawer. Your latest story about the Duchesse de Falloux is ready to be sent to the illegal press for printing."

She blanched. "You got hold of the desk key?"

"On a couple of occasions, yes."

"Dear God . . ." She jerked back, her hand covering her heart. He saw the dawning on her cherished face. "You took it from me in the library, didn't you?" Her bravado cracked, as did her voice. "After what happened in that room, after the intimacy we shared there, you *stole* the key from me?"

Unable to speak, he simply nodded.

She stepped forward and cracked her palm against his cheek. "You are vile!"

Nicolas briefly closed his eyes. He'd never allowed anyone to strike him, but with self-recrimination slicing through him, he'd made no attempt to raise his hands and ward her off, even though he'd seen the blow coming. The sting from her slap was barely noticeable in comparison to the consuming anguish wracking him.

"Henriette, go upstairs and burn everything incriminating in Anne's desk," the Comtesse ordered.

Henriette and Camille rose together.

"I'll help her," Camille said.

Nicolas shook his head. "Burning the contents of her desk won't make a difference. If I don't bring Leduc to the King today, members of the Guard will be here to arrest you all. They are aware that Leduc is among you. You will be interrogated until there is a confession. If the King feels it's warranted, torture can be used, even on a woman."

They looked at him with dread and fright.

What they didn't realize was that those very same emotions were among the many goring his heart.

"I'm sorry," he said. Those words weren't enough and didn't begin to express how he felt. There was so much more he wanted to say—to Anne. He wanted a private moment to talk.

Would she even give him the chance?

"If the King wants Leduc, then that is what we shall give him," the Comtesse announced. "I will tell him I'm Leduc."

Surprised gasps pierced the silence. But no one was more surprised than he. His cold-hearted grandmother, a woman who'd been indifferent toward her own daughter, was willing to take the blame here and spare Anne?

Hope soared inside him. The Comtesse was hardly guiltless in the Leduc matter. This was good. No, this was an excellent solution.

"No, madame, I cannot let you do that," Anne said.

"Nonsense." The Comtesse approached and placed her arm around Anne. "I am your patroness. I encouraged—*strongly encouraged*—you to write these stories. I am not blameless here. And when the King sees me—an old woman—I doubt he'll have the stomach to do much to me."

"I'll say it was me." Henriette spoke up.

"What? No!" Anne shook her head, dismayed.

"Anne." Henriette approached her. "I'm the one who is constantly reminding you how dire our finances are."

"Yes, and I have been a burden, too," Camille said. "Henriette and I have both made it impossible for you to quit, Anne."

"I didn't wish to quit," Anne said. "I still don't intend to quit. I will be the one who appears before the King as Leduc. I will explain to him what I have done and why." Her jaw was set.

Nicolas's heart constricted. "And what will you say? That you have been besmirching the reputation of prominent men because you once suffered a broken heart? Do you think the King—who happens to be a man and prominent—will understand? Let the Comtesse take your place. It is the best option."

Pain seeped back into Anne's eyes. "You know the details of what happened with Roland, too?"

Nicolas approached and stopped before her. "He never deserved your affections."

Tears in her eyes, she squared her shoulders, took in a ragged breath and let it out. In a cold voice she said, "You need to make an arrest today. I will get my things. You will arrest me and only me." She stalked from the room, her sisters on her heels.

Her words knifed into him. He had to reason with her. *Jésus-Christ*, he had to tell her how he felt about her. And that he refused to let anything happen to her.

Nicolas turned to leave.

"Just a moment," the Comtesse de Cottineau said, stepping in front of him. "I'd like a word with you."

"I have more pressing matters to attend to. So if you'll kindly step out of—"

"You searched my desks, I presume," she injected.

"Yes. *So?*"

She nodded. "Then I suppose you read the contents of the yellow box in that desk over there." She gestured toward the ebony and gold desk near the windows.

"You wrote some letters to your daughter. You didn't send them. What of it?"

"There are facts about what happened between your mother and me that I'm certain you're not aware of."

"And I'm not interested in learning about them either."

She sighed. "You despise me, Nicolas. I suppose if I were you, I'd despise me, too. You must have been quite gleeful when you learned I was mixed up with this Leduc matter. Not only could you bring in the elusive Leduc, but you could legitimately sweep me up in the mess, too."

Though prolonging his conversation with his grandmother was the last thing he wanted to do, he couldn't help but ask, "How did you know I was on this mission?"

"I didn't. Not for certain. I knew you'd been appointed to the King's private Guard. When I arrived this morning and was told you were here and that you wanted to forge a relationship with me, I didn't believe it. Given the controversy Leduc's stories have stirred and that you are a Musketeer, it seemed the only logical explanation for your presence was that you were looking for Leduc. I knew you were brighter than most. Other men have tried to locate Leduc and never came close."

He was about to respond when she raised her hand to silence him. "You sent me on a fool's errand, and for that alone, I should be furious with you, not to mention the other things you've done here in the name of your 'mission.' But I'm not angry with you—for two reasons. The first reason is—"

"As I said, I have more pressing—"

"Because you're in love with Anne."

That froze the words on his tongue. *Merde.* Where the hell was she going with this?

"You are suffering, as much as Anne is. I can see the anguish in your eyes. What you have to do is difficult. I'll not condemn you for your actions, for I can see that you are efficiently condemning yourself. I'm sorry you are both in this predicament."

He hadn't expected this—the soft sadness in her gray eyes, the compassion in her tone. This was not the woman he envisioned his grandmother to be.

She gave him a sad smile. "You have my Joséphine's eyes, you know." To his surprise, she touched his cheek. "You look like her. I'm glad. I feared you'd turn out to be like your father."

"No, I am not like my father." His late brother David was.

Her smile turned brighter, seemingly pleased by his answer. "The second reason I'm not angry with you, Nicolas, is because I don't want to make the same mistake with you that I made with your mother. I learned a terrible lesson: words said in anger can cause irreparable damage. I said things to your mother in anger I should never have said. Things I have regretted ever since. I was furious with her for running off and marrying your father. I knew it was a terrible match. And your father loathed me for my low opinion of him. Within a few months of their marriage, I began writing letters to Joséphine, letters of apology, hoping to make amends. I never heard back from her. She ignored them. Ignored me. Never bothered to tell me of the births of her sons. But still I wrote and wrote, hoping that she'd break her silence and forgive me. I was informed of her death by your father. In his letter he also advised me that he'd been intercepting my letters. He returned each and every one to me in the yellow box. Your mother never saw any of them. She went to her grave thinking I hated her." Tears welled in her eyes and quietly slipped down her cheeks.

He was speechless. Every fiber in Nicolas's being told him that what the Comtesse said was true. All of it. His father was just the sort of man who'd do such a thing. Of that he had no doubt.

"What your father did broke my heart, and I'm certain he often broke Joséphine's heart. Though I could not communicate with her, I made certain I was kept abreast of the goings-on in her home. Coin placed in the correct palms will garner much information. I was well aware of his heavy-handed ways, that he kept her isolated in the country, away from me and friends. I knew of your brother's death and of your recent appointment to the Guard." She shook her head. "It is because of your father and men like him that I encouraged Anne to write the kind of stories Leduc writes."

His brows shot up. "My father helped inspire these stories?"

"I'd say your father and Roland d'Orsay were the inspiration, yes. Anne suggested the idea of Leduc and I fully endorsed it. I helped by supplying her with trustworthy women to offer similar tales of woe for Leduc to write about."

The lump in his throat was huge.

"You don't believe me?" she asked quietly.

Nicolas had to clear his throat before he could speak. "I believe you, madame. I know what kind of man my father was and how unhappy he made my mother."

"Well, I must confess that for the first time ever, I find myself unable to utterly despise the man." The Comtesse took his hand. "He sired you. Now that I have you near, I'll not lose you. You are my family. You are all I have left of Joséphine. I hope we can have the relationship I have always prayed for." Fresh tears were in her eyes.

Nicolas's head was spinning. Emotions were inundating him. There was so much to absorb with this newfound information about his grandmother. Feeling discomposed, he held his tongue. But he didn't pull away. Instead, Nicolas squeezed her hand, then covered it with his other.

She smiled through her tears. "Now then, Nicolas, you have some important matters you must attend to—or as you called them, 'pressing matters.' First, you must convince your beloved that you are not the contemptible man she accuses you of being. Next, you'll have to keep her out of prison."

Dieu, why didn't she ask him to part the Red Sea?

*****

Anne waited with her sisters near the carriage to be escorted to Versailles. The day had grayed, and by the angry look of the dark clouds, there was a threat of rain. The gloom inside her was mirrored by the skies. In a few hours she'd be before the King and face the consequences. She was afraid. Terrified. She wouldn't lie about her role as Gilbert Leduc. However, when it came to the women who'd offered their stories to Leduc, she was prepared to do whatever it took to protect their identities.

A gasp from Camille yanked her from her thoughts. The Comtesse and two men wearing the distinct uniform of the King's private Guard were descending the stairs in front of the Comtesse's home. Thomas and Nicolas. It was the first time she'd ever seen them in uniform. Her heart pounded as she took in Nicolas's blue tabard with its silver cross, blue breeches and black boots. His baldric rested on his right shoulder and crossed over his chest to his left hip.

With his powerful form, his confident stride and his fierce expression, he looked intimidating. Dangerous to cross. There was no doubt about it—Nicolas made the perfect King's protector.

The sight of him made her ache. She turned away.

Strong fingers curled around her arm. She was yanked sideways. Suddenly, she was stumbling along behind Nicolas as he dragged her back inside the hôtel. The door slammed shut and he pushed her up against it.

Her mouth fell open, stunned by his actions. She was just about to offer up a few choice words when he crushed his mouth against hers, giving her a hot open-mouth kiss. A mindless rush of desire surged over her. Her knees practically buckled.

She fisted the front of his uniform. *What are you doing? Push him away!* But shamelessly her mouth was still latched to his, and she was trembling.

Abruptly, he pulled away. His strong hands clasped her cheeks, his breathing as quick as hers. "I love you."

Her heart lost a beat.

He released her and pressed his palms against the door on either side of her head. "I love you, Anne. So much. A maddening amount! I'm so very sorry for every lie. All the deceit. And for the pain I've caused you. Knowing that I hurt you is destroying me. I came here to do the King's bidding. I didn't care about you, your sisters, or the Comtesse. You're correct there. I wanted to impress the King. I wanted a promotion. All I ever wanted was to rank highly in the Guard. But you, you have a way of affecting me." He shoved himself off the door. "I have no understanding how you manage it. But you do!"

He placed his hands on his hips and let out a sharp breath. "I'm in love with you and I know you love me. I could tell you wanted to tell me last night. And—*Dieu*—I wanted to hear it."

He stepped closer to her and pulled her into his arms. "I wanted you from the moment I saw you. And yes, I set out to have sex with you. Heated, intensely pleasurable—meaningless—sex. You weren't supposed to matter to me. I wasn't supposed to fall in love with the woman I had to arrest. I'd been walking around for days thinking up excuses not to search your desk for evidence."

He pressed his cheek to her hair. "I don't care about the promotion, or the Guard. If they put you in prison, I'll do whatever it takes to see you freed, including bribing the prison guards and fleeing the country with you. They can take away anything they want, as long as they don't take you from me."

Anne was shaking hard by the time she raised her arms and wrapped them around his neck. Closing her eyes, she buried her face at the base of his throat, inhaling his scent and taking in his warmth. Relishing the strength of his arms as they practically held her up.

Tenderly, he stroked her hair. "Anne, please say something."

She raised her head and gazed up into his beautiful eyes. "You weren't supposed to matter to me either. But . . . I love you." The words came out in a joyful rush, unrestrained. Straight from the heart.

She'd finally found the love and passion she'd always dreamed about.

In a few hours, her world could collapse.

*****

Nicolas's expression was tightly guarded as they waited in the Mars drawing room at Versailles. With Anne, her sisters, and the Comtesse already gripped with fear, he refused to add to their distress by showing any outward signs of the terror he felt.

The occasional sniffle or soft sob from Camille broke the silence, as did the laughter and music that occasionally drifted in from the gardens. Thomas tried consoling Camille as best he could, without success.

The King was in the gardens, as usual. Preferring the outdoors, Louis spent most of his day outside surrounded by courtiers and musicians who followed him around the expansive lawns covered with massive flowerbeds and fountains, bushes and his rare orange trees.

The wait was maddening. How much longer before Louis finally pulled himself away and entered the State Rooms? They'd already waited for what seemed a fucking eternity.

He glanced at Anne. She stood by his side, quiet and brave. He was amazed and proud of her courage. Most would have collapsed under the weight of worry and fright. She shed no tears the way Camille did, nor did she wring her hands as Henriette was doing.

Needing to touch Anne, every once in a while Nicolas reached out and squeezed her hand reassuringly, uncertain if he was trying to reassure her or himself. He would have held her the entire time but the Captain of the Guard, Tristan de Tiersonnier, entered and exited the room frequently.

Nicolas wrestled with the possibilities and probabilities of what the King might do, his restless mind making his heart race. The Mars drawing room offered little by way of diversions. Its walls were a plain red and the ornately painted ceiling depicted various scenes that he didn't want to look at. Especially the one directly overhead. It was Claude Audran's *Mars in a Chariot Drawn by Wolves*. *Le Loup* was a nickname he'd never minded, but rather liked.

Now he disliked it immensely.

A wolf was a predator. He'd come to realize he wasn't that cold. He'd been well on the road to becoming just like his father and brother, and he was grateful that he'd veered off that path, for that path had led him to Anne. To love. And even more surprising, to a grandmother he actually wanted to know more about.

The Comtesse took Anne's other hand. "Anne, I'm too old for this. This wait is taking years off my life. We'll assure the King that Leduc is through. He'll not write again."

Anne glanced at the older woman and then at Nicolas.

"She's right, *chérie*. Leduc is done," he said. "He has to be. Even if the King is in a generous mood, he'll not permit you to keep breaking the law."

Anne gazed straight ahead and then softly ceded. "I know. But who will speak for those women in distress? Leduc was their only voice."

"We'll think of another way to aid women," his grandmother offered. "But it will be legal. Something that won't perturb the King."

The door burst open, causing Anne to jump and Nicolas's heart to lurch. The King and his Captain, Tiersonnier, marched in.

Immediately, Nicolas and Thomas bowed as the women curtsied low.

Louis sighed. "Which one is the author?" he asked Tiersonnier.

Nicolas didn't like the annoyance in the King's tone. His mood wasn't particularly genial today. His fear spiked.

Anne stepped forward. "I am, Sire."

Nicolas wanted to yank her back and shout, "No! There's been a mistake."

Louis cocked a brow, then tilted his head to one side. His gaze moved over Anne, a slow assessment that made Nicolas's nostrils flare and his fists clench. At close to fifty years of age, his King was a notorious womanizer, and the leer he'd directed at Anne gave him great unease.

"Come with me," Louis said, spinning on his heel and stalking from the room. Anne fell into step behind the King.

Nicolas stepped forward, but Tiersonnier shoved his hand against Nicolas's chest. "Not you. Just her. Everyone else waits here." Tiersonnier fell in behind Anne, and slammed the door closed.

Nicolas's heart sank. His ire rose. There were State Rooms on either side of the Mars drawing room. It didn't escape his notice that the King was headed in the direction of his private apartments—*where his bedchamber was located.*

Camille wept openly now, accepting Thomas's shoulder as her sobbing worsened.

Nicolas's mind was besieged with unwanted thoughts far worse than before. Was he supposed to just wait here while the King took Anne and . . . *Merde.* He couldn't finish the thought.

Teeth clenched, he stalked to the window and looked down at the north gardens. But all he saw were the images flashing in his mind of Anne in the King's bed. He slammed his fist against the wall.

"Nicolas." His grandmother placed her hand on his shoulder. "I know what you're thinking but you mustn't torture yourself so. Anne is an intelligent woman. She's been propositioned by powerful men before. She knows how to be tactful, yet to the point."

"She's never had to refuse a King."

"I believe in her, Nicolas, and so should you," she countered.

"I do believe in her. But I know Louis's vice-ridden ways," he said tightly. He was a thousand times a fool. He should have fled the country with her and never brought her to the King. His duty be damned. Thoughts of racing down to the State apartments after Anne were rioting in his head. How difficult would it be to get past the guards normally stationed in front of the King's private chambers? How would he get her out of there if he managed to breach the King's security?

The doors swung open, ensnaring Nicolas's attention.

Tiersonnier stood at the threshold. "Follow me." He turned and left.

The Captain of the Guard led them through more State Rooms, down the stairwell, and eventually to the doors leading out to the gardens.

"Are the King and Mademoiselle de Vignon outside?" Nicolas asked.

"No," was all Tiersonnier offered.

Nicolas wasn't about to relent. "Will the mademoiselle be escorted to the gardens to where her family is waiting?" He needed answers. He was about ready to jump out of his skin.

"If that is what His Majesty chooses." Tiersonnier was a large, imposing man, only a few years older than Nicolas and beyond irritating.

"Do you have any idea how long her family will have to wait out in the gardens before His Majesty 'chooses'?"

Eyes narrowed, Tiersonnier stepped in close, a gesture meant to intimidate, knowing he had a deterring effect on the men in the Guard. But Nicolas was neither deterred nor intimidated. He glared back, wanting nothing more than to deliver his fist against the man's arrogant jaw.

"Savignac, you'd do well to remember not to question your superiors. You'll wait in the gardens as ordered by the King until you are told otherwise."

"Of course, Captain," Thomas said, yanking Nicolas away and shoving him out the door.

Outside in the gardens, the noise from the throng abraded Nicolas's jangled nerves. He tried to maintain his composure, but he couldn't stop thinking, as his eyes scanned the windows on the upper floor—where the King's private apartments were located. Anne was alone up there, with their lascivious monarch.

Was the King striking a bargain with her? Her freedom for a fuck? Worse still, what if Louis asked her to be his next mistress? Versailles would become her gilded prison. And until the King lost interest, she'd be lost to Nicolas.

"Forget about it, Nicolas," Thomas murmured in his ear. "You can't go back in there."

"Anne!" Camille gasped.

Nicolas snapped his head around, searching the crowd, his heart suddenly pounding in his throat. He caught sight of her brilliant red hair as she maneuvered through the throng.

She was alone. Her expression was unreadable.

Forcing his legs to eat up the distance between them, he grabbed her by the shoulders the moment he reached her. "What happened?"

Her sisters, Thomas, and the Comtesse grouped around her, insulating her from the scores of people around them.

"It seems that the King is about as fond of the male aristocracy as Leduc is," Anne said, sotto voce.

"What do you mean?" Henriette asked.

"He told me that he *enjoyed* the stories. He wanted to know the author behind them."

Camille placed her hand on Anne's arm. *"Enjoyed?* He really said that?"

Anne nodded. "He has a great dislike for many of the men I depicted in the pen portraits and found the volumes amusing. He confided that since the Fronde, he hasn't had much regard for the men in the upper class. And he liked it that Leduc turned out to be both a woman and French."

The Comtesse let out a laugh. *"Ah,* the Fronde, of course! Louis was still a boy, not yet old enough to rule, when his cousin and many noblemen rose up against him, almost dethroning him. It happened before any of you were born. It was a horrible uprising against the Crown. In fact, he and his mother had to flee Paris in the middle of the night and live in exile until the country could be brought back to order."

"Well, he's not forgotten the ordeal, I can assure you," Anne said. "It has colored the way he looks at men of power."

"What does this mean?" Nicolas asked. "Are you free to go?"

A beautiful radiant smile formed on her lips. "Yes. But I am forbidden to write any more stories by Leduc. He gave me praise and a warning."

Nicolas let out a whoop of joy and pulled her into his arms. He didn't care who was watching. He just wanted to hold her, the tension and fear draining from his body.

Then a thought struck him.

He pulled her away. "Excuse us," he told the others, clasped her hand and strode off, stopping several feet away from their group and the crowd. Holding her by the shoulders, he asked, "Did the King try to . . . Did he . . . proposition you?"

She lifted a brow. "Oh. Yes. He did." Her tone was flippant.

"*And?*"

A smile twitched on her lips. "I'm not going to be the next royal mistress, Nicolas—if I get a better offer, that is." Mischief twinkled in her eyes. She was clearly enjoying herself at his expense.

He pulled her to him and dipped his head, her smile contagious. "You're being very naughty, Anne," he murmured in her ear, his cock swelling between them. "Perhaps I'll take you home and tie you to my bed and keep you bound for my pleasure. That way there can be no other man."

"Perhaps the only offer I'll accept is having you tied to my bed, bound for my pleasure."

He laughed. "Anne de Vignon, you are mine. I love you." He kissed her, enjoying the silky warmth of her mouth.

By the end of the kiss, her cheeks were a pretty pink, a small sign that she was already heated from their short exchange. "I love you, too. With all my heart. And I'm going to help those women somehow, Nicolas."

He brushed an errant red curl off her cheek. "I know you are, and I fully support it, as long as you stay away from the King."

She placed her hands on his chest. "I'm also going to write a lot more poetry."

He grinned. "The world will be enriched by them."

Anne's smile grew and she slipped her arms around his waist. "And what are your plans for the future, sir?"

He lowered his head and brushed his lips lightly over the sensitive spot under her ear, enjoying her soft gasp. "I intend to marry one very beautiful redheaded poetess and spend the rest of my days loving her and cherishing her mind, spirit and heart."

A Historical Tidbit

Before you decide that Anne was released too easily, let me assure you this is *exactly* how King Louis XIV would have behaved.

Without a doubt, he was an intimidating figure. But it seemed he had a soft spot for clever women. There were a number of them during his reign that he admired. Whenever he learned that a woman bested any man of the upper class—either with her wit, or her abilities with a sword, (you'll learn more about that in *Bewitching in Boots*;)—he delighted in it. He would have liked our heroine, Anne de Vignon, very much.

The *Fronde*—the civil uprising that started when Louis was only ten years old—scarred Louis for life.

Incited by power-hungry nobles, they almost dethroned their boy King. They prompted riots in the streets, had the palace stormed—until finally one night young Louis and his mother were forced to flee Paris and live in exile for a while. He never forgot the hardship and fear he and his mother endured during that time. He developed a lifelong dislike and mistrust for the aristocracy. Intent on being absolute ruler, he spent his reign intimidating them. In fact, his distrust was one of the reasons that years later he moved his court out of Paris and built Versailles. He brilliantly kept the upper class under his roof.

And his control.

Seventeenth century France was beyond elegant, and refined—with its theaters and ballets, its salons for the intellectually elite, and of course its extravagant masked balls. I just couldn't resist bringing to life a little bit of the publishing world of the time—where pen portraits were all the rage.

It was during this same time period that fairy tales were born—thanks to French writer Charles Perrault, creator of *The Tales of Mother Goose*, (and the genre of modern day fairy tales). While attending the very same sorts of salons mentioned in *Little Red Writing*, he went on to write stories that have delighted people for centuries: *Sleeping Beauty, Little Red Riding Hood, Puss in Boots, Bluebeard,* and the ever-popular *Cinderella,* to name a few.

This novella is loosely based on Little Red Riding Hood. I hope you enjoyed Little Red Writing!

Glossary

Antechamber	The sitting room in a lord's or lady's private apartments (chambers).
Caleçons	Drawers/underwear.
Chambers	Another word for private apartments. A lord's or lady's chambers consisted of a bedroom, a sitting room, a bathroom, and a *cabinet* (office). Some chambers were bigger and more elaborate than others. Some cabinets were so large, they were used for private meetings.
Chère	Dear one. (French endearment for a woman, *cher* for a man).
Chérie	Darling or cherished one. (French endearment for a woman, *chéri* for a man).
Comte/Comtesse	Count/Countess.
Dieu	God.
Duc/Duchesse	Duke/Duchess.
Fronde	A civil uprising from 1648—1653. Incited by ambitious nobles, they almost dethroned their boy King.

(Louis was only ten years old when it began.) He developed a lifelong dislike and mistrust for the aristocracy. Intent on being absolute ruler, he spent his reign intimidating them.

Hôtel/Château The upper class and the wealthy bourgeois (middle class) often had a city mansion in Paris (*hôtel*) in addition to their palatial country estate(s) (*château*).

Justacorps A fitted knee-length coat, worn over a man's vest and breeches.

Lettre de Cachet Orders/letters of confinement—without trial—signed by the King with the royal seal (*cachet*).

Merde Shit.

Nom de plume Pen name.

Salle Room

Salle de Bain Bathroom. A small room located in one's private apartments/chambers in either a château or hôtel. The room usually had a fireplace, a tub, and a toilet (that looked like a chair with a chamber pot). The room was small on purpose so that the fire from the fireplace would keep the space warm while one bathed.

Salle de Buffet Dining Room.

Seigneur Dieu Lord God.

READ AN EXCERPT OF BEWITCHING IN BOOTS

Inspired by the tale of Puss in Boots—an erotically charged historical romance novella from the acclaimed Fiery Tales series.

Elisabeth de Roussel, daughter of the King, is accustomed to getting what she wants—and she wants gorgeous Tristan de Tiersonnier, Count of Saint-Marcel, the ex-commander of the King's elite private Guard.

A recent injury has forced Tristan to leave his distinguished position. But Elisabeth is determined to make him see he's every bit the man he once was—and more than man enough for her...

BEWITCHING IN BOOTS

Moral of the Story of Puss in Boots:

"If a man has quick success
In winning such a fair princess,
By turning on the charm,
Then regard his manners, looks, and dress,
That inspired her deepest tenderness,
For they can't do one any harm."

Charles Perrault (1628–1703)

CHAPTER ONE

"Do you *really* think your plan will work, Elisabeth?" Claire swiped a curl from her damp forehead. The summer breeze stealing its way into their moving carriage was a mixed blessing. It offered some relief from the heat, but brought with it wafts of dust.

This wasn't the most comfortable trip Elisabeth de Roussel had ever taken, but it was the most important—to her. "For the third time, yes." Her voice was calm, belying the disquiet she felt. Her nerves jangled; she didn't need her sister to keep repeating the same question.

"You're going to seduce Tristan de Tiersonnier, a man who makes other men quake with fear and women tremble with desire. And you're going to do it, dressed like *that?*"

"That is the plan." Elisabeth glanced over at her maid, Agathe, and caught her rolling her eyes. Elisabeth fully expected the older woman to voice her dissent over the plan, but instead Agathe was uncharacteristically quiet, and stared out the window, lips pursed.

Claire leaned in. "Elisabeth, you are dressed like a *man*. A shirt, breeches, black boots—those are men's clothes. Well, perhaps not *those* black boots. No man would wear something so snug around his calves."

"I'm quite aware of how I'm dressed, dear sister." Her younger sibling didn't need to know what an utter mess Elisabeth was inside, nor was she going to admit that she was dressed this way because she wanted—needed—her prized sword at her hip. It gave her confidence. Helped to bolster courage. And courage was what she'd need to execute her plan.

Especially when the plan centered on the only man who intimidated her. The imposing sinfully beautiful former commander of the King's private Guard—the Musketeers— Tristan de Tiersonnier, Comte de Saint-Marcel.

One look from his intense blue eyes and she was undone— when no man shook her, not even her father, the King. By doing nothing more than walking into a room, Tristan commanded her attention and ignited her senses—reducing her into some gawking unsophisticated ingénue. With his confident manner, his tall and powerful body, he exuded authority. And—God help her—such potent sensuality. He made her ache. Heart and body.

He burned in her blood.

Sadly, nothing had lessened her fever for Tristan. Not marriage to another man. Not the lovers she'd taken since the Duc's death. Not time or distance.

"I'm all for being a part of one of your schemes, Elisabeth," Claire said. "In fact, I'd never refuse. They're far too much fun. But this one is rather involved."

That was an understatement.

Claire had no idea just how involved her plan was or what Elisabeth truly hoped to accomplish during this sojourn, but she couldn't explain all of it to her sister. Claire always looked up to her. As much as she adored Claire, Elisabeth couldn't reveal to her, or anyone, just how vulnerable she was to Tristan.

It was a weakness. She never showed her weaknesses. One didn't survive at court by being transparent—ever.

And Elisabeth had survived plenty of attempts to diminish her, both at court and in the eyes of the King. Her late mother had taught her well. She'd been a fine example of how strength and a cunning mind benefited a woman. She hadn't kept the

King's interest longer than any of his other mistresses without knowing a thing or two about how to be clever in a man's world. Elisabeth had adopted her mother's finesse and fortitude and had risen among the brood sired by His Majesty to become the favorite royal daughter. And she used her favored position to protect Claire—who went mostly unnoticed and unprotected by their father— from the constant courtly intrigue.

"*Hrrmph* . . . Seems like a lot of trouble to go to just to bed a man," Agathe mumbled. "We could have stayed home. There are plenty of men at Versailles to choose from."

"There are indeed," Elisabeth said. Her period of mourning over, during the last year she'd had her choice of lovers. Had the freedom to pick and choose whom she wanted. She'd enjoyed the freedom that came with widowhood.

But her freedom was running out.

If she was going to do something about Tristan, it had to be now.

"The men at court bore me," Elisabeth added, affecting her usual tone. One that was purposely blasé. One that gave the world the impression she was indifferent to all things. "The timing is perfect. Veronique is no longer Tristan's mistress. This is the most opportune time."

Claire crinkled her nose. "Veronique . . ." she muttered with disdain. A disdain shared by Elisabeth for their unscrupulous half-sister, the court filled with too many just like her.

"Opportune?" Agathe snorted. "Perhaps Madame has forgotten that the man was dismissed from his position as Captain of the Guard—and the reason why?"

"I haven't forgotten, Agathe," Elisabeth said, "and it is not a permanent situation. Tristan is strong and skilled. Sooner or later His Majesty will reinstate him." She'd see to it. It was part of her plan, important for many reasons, including thwarting Veronique's ambitions. Three months ago, Tristan had been injured in the line of duty. For two and a half months he'd convalesced at the palace until the King, acting on the advice of the royal physicians who felt Tristan would never completely heal, had replaced him as Captain of the Guard.

"So how do you plan on seducing him?" Claire asked, her eyes twinkling with mischief.

Elisabeth smiled. "Now where would be the fun in telling you that? You'll just have to wait and see." She had no idea how she was going to go about seducing Tristan. Her mother had taught her how to entice men, what they liked in and out of the boudoir. But Tristan was not like any man she'd ever known. He wasn't the sort of man who could be led around by the nose. He wouldn't be easily lured.

Claire frowned. "I will still get to help, yes?"

"Of course. That's why I brought you along." Elisabeth glanced at Agathe. "I'm going to need both of you to help."

Her old and faithful servant looked about as thrilled over the prospect as she'd be at developing a body rash.

"Excellent." Claire beamed. "I do so admire your bravery, Elisabeth. Normally women wait to be approached by Tristan de Tiersonnier. You're the only woman I know who is willing to approach him. He's a little too serious, a little too intense for me. I've always found him to be rather unnerving."

So did she. For entirely different reasons: the unbreakable pull he had on her and the desire she had for him that was far too keen. *If all goes well, you might have him tonight . . .* Her nerve endings quivered with life, the notion as thrilling as it was terrifying. It took all she possessed not to abort her plan and race back to Versailles. But she couldn't. Wouldn't. It was time to take control and sate the tormenting carnal hunger she had for this man—who'd barely noticed her and had only spoken to her out of duty.

Well, today he'd notice her.

Acting on the signs she'd read in her father, on the subtle comments he'd made, Elisabeth knew he'd select a new husband for her soon. She'd be trapped in another marriage filled with lonely nights fantasizing about Tristan. More lonely years spent starved for his touch, his taste.

She wouldn't go through that again.

If she was going to be forced to marry once more, then her husband may as well be Tristan. A husband of her choosing. If she failed to seduce him into the idea of marriage, then at the very least she wouldn't fail to seduce him into her bed for a week of unbridled sex. It was unwise, utterly foolhardy, for a woman to crave a man as intensely as she craved Tristan. To be as spellbound as she was by him. Her mother had taught her better than that. One way or another, husband or lover, he'd bed her and she'd at last satisfy this hunger, snap this fascination, and purge him from her heart, body and soul.

She'd never find any contentment in her life—know any peace—if she didn't break the power Tristan had over her.

"I find Tiersonnier appealing," Elisabeth remarked. "And as for his 'intensity,' I think that could be put to good use in the boudoir."

Claire giggled. "Too true, sister."

Agathe pursed her lips firmer together.

Elisabeth's plan was simple. Before she could marry Tristan, she had to convince both the King and Tristan that the irresistible ex-commander of the Musketeers was her perfect match.

There were only two problems with her plan. One, the King saw Tristan as infirm and not fit to marry her. And two, Tristan wasn't going be easy to seduce into her bed, much less into marriage.

He hated her.

The carriage stopped. Her entourage of Musketeers and a second carriage filled with Elisabeth's and Claire's trunks and necessities halted as well.

Elisabeth alighted from the carriage with the help of one of the King's Guardsmen. Her stomach dropped at the sight before her.

"Good Lord, Elisabeth, is that Tiersonnier's château?" her sister asked, stopping by her side.

Agathe simply shook her head in dismay.

Standing in the courtyard, overgrown with weeds, was an old two-story country mansion, its stone masonry crumbling in many spots. The once proud mythical statues adorning its rooftops were blackened with dirt and age.

Elisabeth took a deep breath and let it out slowly. "It's in some need of repair."

Agathe snorted. "That is putting it mildly."

This isn't a setback. She wasn't going to be discouraged by the state of Tristan's abode or, more important, what it suggested about the finances of the lord of this château and how that diminished her already slim chances of being with Tristan beyond the week. She'd come this far. She'd forge ahead.

She'd simply add to the plan. What was one more obstacle in her path? After all, she was already attempting the impossible. In addition to convincing the King that Tristan was capable of commanding His Majesty's Guard once more, and making Tristan want her, clearly she'd have to convince her father that Tristan was richer than he was.

She was wearing her lucky boots. Good thing.

She was going to need all the luck she could get.

*****

"Is this what you do all day? Sit in the library?" Gabriel de Tiersonnier asked with a smile as he strolled into the room.

Seated on the settee, his leg propped up, Tristan stared out at the gardens. Without glancing at his brother, he responded dryly, "No. Sometimes I sit in the salon." His tone was caustic. Embittered.

He wanted to be left alone and tried to ignore his brother and his good mood. It was as infuriating as the unrelenting dull ache in Tristan's leg. An incessant reminder of his debilitated state. All these weeks and no bloody sign of improvement. He still walked with a cane. He still couldn't make peace with his crippled limb. He hadn't wanted to believe the royal physicians' prognosis. Now he was beginning to lose hope of a complete recovery. And his frustration and fury over it mounted daily.

Still smiling, Gabriel shook his head and sat down in a nearby chair, making himself comfortable.

Merde. His brother meant to stay.

"Really, Tristan, this sedate existence of yours is as exciting as living among celibate monks."

"You should know. You were one of them, until they tossed you out last week." Gabriel had returned two days ago, shattering Tristan's solitude, and he resented it.

He resented just about everything nowadays. He resented how far he'd fallen for a man who had it all—command of the most prestigious, most elite corps in the realm, the ear of the King and his esteem, magnificent apartments at Versailles, and a number of women to bed whenever he chose, including his favorite, Veronique. But his favorite turned out to be a conniving little opportunist, who was quick to leave. The moment he was replaced as Captain of the Musketeers, she was bedding his successor.

What did he have left when all the dust had settled? A lame leg. A broken-down château he cared nothing about. And worse, staid empty years stretched out before him—a life so contrary to his active existence. He'd fought in countless campaigns for his country during his distinguished military career. He'd risen through the ranks to eventually head the King's private Guard, and had conducted covert operations and quashed conspiracies while in charge of the safety and protection of the royal family.

Gabriel chuckled good-naturedly. "I was not a monk, and well you know it. I was in the seminary. I hadn't taken any vows yet. Our dear departed father felt he needed to have one son in the service of God. I told him it was a mistake to send me."

"I suppose 'our dear departed father' overestimated your restraint. Here you thought celibacy was a mere suggestion and not a requirement for a man studying to become a member of the Holy Church."

"Exactly." Gabriel grinned. "Glad you see my point."

"Yes, and who knew they'd take it so seriously when they caught you with two women at the same time—twice."

Gabriel laughed. "Ah, now Tristan, those women were well worth being expelled from the seminary. Who needs to wait to die to go to paradise when a man can sample those four lovelies right here on earth?"

"Tristan." His uncle Richard de Tiersonnier entered the room, his brow furrowed. "Are you expecting a Duc?"

"A Duc?" he repeated. "Of course not, why?" No one from court had visited him since his departure from the royal palace. He'd been well forgotten in mere weeks—after years of loyal service to the King and his family.

"There is a six-horse carriage among the entourage outside."

Tristan was baffled. Entourage? A six-horse carriage was definitely a Duc. What Duc? Why was he here?

Grabbing his cane, he struggled to his feet, refusing help from Gabriel, and made his way to the courtyard to greet his notable visitor, his uncle and brother falling in behind him.

Tristan arrested his steps outside the main entrance of his château. Two carriages, one with six white horses, and thirty of his former men each on horseback filled his courtyard.

But if that wasn't enough, by far the most astonishing sight was the King's favorite daughter, Elisabeth, Duchesse de Roussel. Flanked by her maid and her sister, she stood not twenty feet away dressed in breeches, black boots and a white shirt—male clothing custom-fitted to her form.

And she looked like anything but a man.

Her breeches accentuated her mouth-watering curves, black boots—like none he'd ever seen—molded to her slender calves, and then there was her shirt. The breeze fluttered the white material, teasing him with glimpses of creamy skin above her breasts. He felt his prick harden.

Tristan clenched his teeth. *Jésus-Christ*, he hadn't had sex since his injury. He'd definitely gone too long without a good fuck if the sight of the King's most spoiled offspring, dressed in men's clothing, was stiffening his cock.

"Where is the Duc?" his uncle asked.

Gabriel stepped around Tristan. "Never mind that, Uncle. Who is that woman dressed in breeches?"

"One of His Majesty's illegitimate daughters." Tristan couldn't keep the disdain from his tone.

"I thought he legitimized all his children born to his mistresses," Richard stated.

"He did. He gave them status and arranged powerful matches for them, too," Tristan said. "This is one of the more self-indulgent among those in the royal brood."

Tightening his jaw, he made his way across the courtyard, hating it that his former men had tso see him hobbling like a cripple. Whatever Elisabeth wanted, he'd refuse. Whatever game she was playing—and it was obvious she was up to no good— he wouldn't engage in it.

He was going to send her and her entourage straight back to Versailles.

Want to know more about BEWITCHING IN BOOTS? Visit www.liladipasqua.com.

THANK YOU for reading LITTLE RED WRITING!

Want my next release for just **99¢?** Sign up for my **99¢ New Release Alert** newsletter at www.LilaDiPasqua.com. Each new release will be **99¢** for a SHORT time only. Get notified. Don't miss out!

FIERY TALES SERIES

Novellas
Sleeping Beau
Little Red Writing
Bewitching in Boots
The Marquis's New Clothes
The Lovely Duckling
The Princess and the Diamonds

Holiday Novella
The Duke's Match Girl

Anthologies
Awakened by a Kiss
The Princess in His Bed

Full-length novels
A Midnight Dance
Undone
Three Reckless Wishes

Lila DiPasqua is a *USA TODAY* bestselling author of historical romance with heat. She lives with her husband, three children and two rescued dogs and is a firm believer in the happily-ever-after. You can find her on Facebook, Twitter, Instagram, and Goodreads!